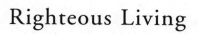

# Righteous Living

# RIGHTEOUS LIVING

stories by

Maureen Hull

TURNSTONE PRESS

Turnstone Press
607–100 Arthur Street
Artspace Building
Winnipeg, Manitoba
Canada    R3B 1H3
www.TurnstonePress.com

Turnstone Press gratefully acknowledges the assistance of the
Canada Council for the Arts, the Manitoba Arts Council and the Government
of Canada through the Book Publishing Industry Development Program for
our publishing activities.

Le Conseil des Arts  The Canada Council
DU CANADA   FOR THE ARTS
DEPUIS 1957   SINCE 1957

These stories have appeared in *Amethyst Review, Chatelaine, Fiddlehead, Fireweed,
Other Voices, Pottersfield Portfolio, Room of One's Own.*

The author gratefully acknowledges the assistance of the Canada
Council for the Arts (Explorations Program) and the support and
encouragement of David Harding.

Cover artwork: detail of original quilt *Journey* by Kathleen Hull

Design: Manuela Dias

Author photograph: Findlay Muir

This book was printed and bound in Canada by
Hignell Book Printing for Turnstone Press.

Canadian Cataloguing in Publication Data

Hull, Maureen, 1949–

Righteous living

ISBN 0-88801-232-2

I. Title.

PS8565.U542R54  1999      C813'.54      C99-920083-6
PR9199.3.H78R54  1999

*To David, Amy and Moira with love*

# Table of Contents

# Bootleggers

Mary Theresa and I searched for bootleggers for years. March and April we looked for footprints in the snow under spruce and fir; in summer we waded the streams, scanning the banks for a dropped butt or twigs broken at suspicious angles. Hunting season put an end to our rambling; we'd heard the stories of people in brown coats shot to death as they hurried home through orchards, parks or woods at dusk, at dawn, in broad daylight. We stayed in our own backyards then, wore red hats and waited until spring came again.

I had a brother, four years older, who told people he was an only child; Mary Theresa had four older brothers and an ever-increasing number of younger brothers and sisters. I liked to rock the little ones. When they were fussy and wouldn't sleep I would sit with them in the old painted rocker, one foot under me for balance and one out to push against the stove. Each baby liked a different speed; you had to find the right one to make it dizzy and quiet. Too slow and it got mad and yelled and turned red, too fast and it got scared and threw up. So some I waltzed and some I barrelled down gravel roads.

"You're the clear ticket for a cranky little one, dear," Mrs. MacInnes praised me.

"She thumps them on their heads to knock them out, Ma," said Mary Theresa.

"Don't you be so foolish. This one's a born mother, unlike yourself, Mary Theresa. I swear you've got the maternal instinct of a cabbage."

I wanted a baby in our house but when I mentioned it, Mother rolled her eyes and said two were quite enough. Did I want her to look like Mrs. MacInnes? Mrs. MacInnes had spidery arms and legs and a large stomach that sagged low just after she'd had a baby and pushed up and out when she was about to have another. The oldest of a large family, she spent a lot of time on the phone with her sisters and cousins giving advice on colic, diaper rash and croup. A cigarette wiggled in the corner of her mouth as she talked. There were burn holes all down the front of her smocks from falling ash.

Joey was the only one of Mary Theresa's older brothers to pay any attention to Mary Theresa and me. He showed us how to make a whistle from a blade of grass, to construct a bow and arrow with string and alder shoots. He built campfires and gave us marshmallows to roast. Once he gave me a whole chocolate bar. I offered to trade my brother, my Patti Page cutouts and a month's allowance for Joey but Mary Theresa refused.

Joey's favourite pastime was looking for bootleggers in the woods, and, originally, we took it up to be with him. Making and selling moonshine was a small but thriving industry in our part of the country. It was a way to make money when the mines were closed and there was no other work to be had. We kids were told to stay out of the woods, in case we tumbled into a pit or bothered the men going about their business. Joey occasionally let us follow him if we were quiet and obeyed orders. He knew the woods for several miles back of town; he kept a compass in his shirt pocket, and a hunting knife in a sheath buckled onto his belt. We carried fishing poles to disguise our true purpose.

"They probably won't believe we're looking for a stream anyway," Mary Theresa cautioned.

"What will they do?"

"Kill us," she said. "Strangle us and bury us in the woods so we

2

won't squeal to the RCMP. There was a boy, over at Bull River, got caught by bootleggers and was missing three months! They wouldn't never have found him, only a beagle out with some hunters found his hand sticking out of the ground when they was looking for rabbits. It was all chewed."

We paused a few moments to savour the horror.

"What if I promised on the Bible not to tell?"

"Ha!" she scoffed. "You think they'd care about a Bible? They'd throw you in a pit so's you'd never be found. A beagle couldn't find you. Not even a bloodhound!"

"But . . . ," I began.

"Shut up or go home," Joey said.

Once Joey showed us a leaf-covered pit filled with burlap bags. He opened one and pulled out a bottle. I wanted to run before the bootleggers found us but Joey and Mary Theresa were poking about, scoffing and bragging, and I knew if I whined they'd never take me with them again. Joey said he might take it and get drunk or maybe sell it and buy a new tire for his bike. Mary Theresa was dirty-double-daring him to do it; I was trying not to pee my pants. By the time they quit fooling around, put the bottle back and scuffed the leaves over the top, it was past suppertime. I was so grateful not to be dead and buried in the woods that I didn't cry when my mother smacked me for being late and dirty.

Every New Year's Eve, my parents threw a house party for the neighbours. There were trays of crackers and olives, devilled eggs and celery logs, bowls of nuts, chips and candy, a huge cheese ball rolled in walnuts and flavoured with brandy. My father set up a bar in the kitchen with ice and mix and bottles of real liquor from the Liquor Commission. He spent the night there, shirt sleeves rolled up, asking everybody, "What's your poison?"

Mother would drink and smoke and dance once with each of the husbands. I watched her carefully and left the party from time to time to practise in front of my bedroom mirror with a cigarette filched from someone's open pack. I didn't light it; that wasn't the point. Shake the cigarette from the pack. Angle the head to light the cigarette with a long and slender, black-and-gold monogrammed lighter. Toss back the head and slowly exhale. Delicately pick bits of tobacco from the tongue with perfect crimson nails—I only swiped non-filters because I particularly liked this bit—return cigarette to lips, inhale, repeat. I rehearsed until the cigarette was a wet lump to be flushed down the toilet. Some day I meant to smoke with just such assured elegance and leave a trail of red-lipsticked butts in heavy crystal ashtrays.

I was always surprised to find Mother and Mrs. MacInnes in a corner, cigarettes and drinks in hand, their heads thrown apart and drawn together by gusts of laughter and whispered conversation. What could they find so amusing to talk about? Mother wasn't just being polite, they were having a good time. Somewhere in their past, they had been girls together. Strands of that old bond lay between them, gathered up after a couple of ryes and a few laughs, pulled tight for an evening, let fall the next day. I wondered if their parents had discouraged their friendship as they grew older. Parents didn't like teen-age girls of different religions to get too close, in case they started up with each other's brothers. That's what they said—started up.

"Did you hear about the MacKenzie girl? She's started up with that Billy Fraser from Benton Street." As if they were climbing a mountain in poor weather without suitable equipment. It was because of the marriage thing. If a Protestant married a Catholic, he or she had to "turn." It seemed rather high-handed on the part of the Catholics, but I admired how handily and how often they pulled it off.

I always fell asleep before midnight. I tried and tried to stay awake but I could never do it. The party would be roaring in my ears and then suddenly the sun would be shining in the window and I would be in my bed, still in my party dress, with my shoes off and a quilt pulled up to my shoulders. Midnight would have come and gone, the firecrackers set off, Mr. Donahue would have made his crank call to complain about the car horns and I would have missed it all again.

Mr. Donahue was the only person on the street who never came to our New Year's Eve party. My mother invited him once but he was so rude to her about my brother and me walking across his backyard that she swore he'd never set foot in her house, supposing he had a heart attack right outside the door.

"The ambulance attendants can just scrape him up off the sidewalk," she said briskly. When Mrs. Donahue ran away, no one felt sorry for him.

"Good for her," said my mother. "I didn't think she had it in her. Poor little thing. I'm sure he beat her. He certainly starved her."

After his wife left, Mr. Donahue got Bruno. Part boxer, part shepherd, brown and black with long legs, small eyes and too many sharp teeth. Stupid and mean. Bruno was supposed to keep the kids from shortcutting across the yard, breaking the lilac branches and killing the grass. He was so vicious he had to be kept on a chain but the chain was on a line so he could run back and forth and patrol the whole yard.

"That dog is going to hurt somebody," said my father. "You kids stay away from him."

Mr. Donahue must have got Bruno for free; he wouldn't have paid. He didn't buy dog food, fed him potatoes and day-old bread with bacon grease.

"He's so tight he squeaks when he walks," said Mrs. MacInnes, and it's true that the year my brother had a paper route, Mr. Donahue always paid in pennies and never on time. After his wife had been gone awhile, his clothes began to fall apart. He bought an old tweed coat from the Salvation Army and hemmed it himself with big stitches in red yarn. The older kids made fun of him, called him "Screwy Louie" because his first name was Lewis, but I was scared of him and terrified of Bruno. Even Mary Theresa said they made her nervous. We figured if Bruno ever got loose he'd eat the first person in his path. Nobody walked on Mr. Donahue's grass anymore; it grew back over the shortcut but the yard was all covered in dog shit and stank so it didn't seem like much of an improvement.

I was coming home from Brownies the day Bruno broke his chain and got me. Mary Theresa was home with the flu and I was dawdling along by myself, smashing shell ice in the puddles. I heard

Joey yell and turned around to see Bruno racing out of the bushes, low and fast and not making a sound. I got my arm up in front of my face but my legs wouldn't move; everything was glued in place. Joey was running towards me from a long way away and Bruno's teeth were deep in my coat; he was shaking his head back and forth and I was starting to fall. Joey hit him on the top of his head, just above where his eyes were hating me like red knives. The eyes went flat and black, and then Bruno and I were together on the ground; still neither one of us had made a sound. Joey yanked the dog away from me but the wet yellow teeth were tangled in the torn fabric of my winter coat and the long sleeve of my Brownie uniform. He unhooked the teeth, then bashed the head a couple of times more with the rock he'd scooped up from beside the road as he was running towards us. He stood over me, breathing hard; then we both saw blood seeping into my sleeve and my arm began to hurt horribly. I shook and sobbed and Joey tried to get me to stand up.

"Don't go soft on me now," he said. "Dog's dead and you're all right. C'mon. I'll walk you home."

He wrapped my scarf tight around my arm and marched me along. He told me minister, priest and rabbi jokes the whole way so that even as I was seeing Bruno's red eyes and yellow teeth and crying, I was laughing because the jokes were so stupid and because Joey wanted me to and I'd have done anything in the world to please him.

The newspaper printed his picture under the heading "LOCAL BOY SAVES YOUNG GIRL FROM VICIOUS ATTACK." There was a story about the rock and how I'd had to have stitches. Joey'd undoubtedly saved my life, the article said.

My mother gave him a kiss and told everybody what an extraordinarily brave young man he was. My father gave him money and said Donahue should have been run out of town years ago. I pinned the clipping up on my wall and read it every night for weeks. Mr. Donahue was fined and then he got another vicious dog. Someone shot it while he was asleep. He got a third one, so mean, people said even he was afraid of it, and then he sat up nights with a shotgun, guarding his guard dog. Somehow it was poisoned. Mr. Donahue was furious, especially when the Mounties said they didn't have enough evidence to charge anyone. Finally Mr. Donahue sold his house and moved away.


I was watching Mother dress for church.

"Mrs. MacInnes sure has a lot of children."

"Yes, and she's a wreck. That poor girl has no peace from one year to the next."

Mother stabbed through her hat and hair with a six-inch-long pin. One end was a large jet bead, the other a sharpened steel point. She tied the ends of a fine silk veil behind her, leaving a mist of delicate velvet dots across her face. She was so lovely, so sophisticated. I wanted to be like her so much I was dizzy.

"She should tell that selfish husband of hers to keep his hands to himself," she muttered.

"Yes, she should," I agreed, hoping for enlightenment. Mother gave me a sharp look and grabbed a brush from the bureau.

"I've told you time and again to brush underneath." She ripped through my hair, picking and pulling until the knots were gone and tears were streaming down my face.

"Too many pregnancies are bad for a woman's health. Get in the car and don't touch anything with those white gloves."

I went out to the car.


"Why doesn't your mother tell your father to stop giving her babies?"

Mary Theresa was shocked. "She can't do that. That's a sin. It's her duty."

"It's not my mother's duty."

"Yes but you're not Catholic and you're going to hell." This was just something we said, in case adults were lurking nearby, trying to catch us out. Privately, we had worked out a deal with God that involved the creation of parallel heavens, one for good Catholics, one for good Protestants. There would be non-denominational get-togethers around the throne on weekends. We also imagined a sort of metaphysical backyard fence that we could lean across to chat.

I had only one minister but Mary Theresa had three priests. Father Cameron was old and didn't do much except help with Mass on holidays. Mostly he watched the big colour TV at the Glebe house with the sound turned up so loud you could hear it in the classrooms at St. Mike's on warm days when the windows were open. *As the World Turns* was his favourite. It was the biggest colour TV in all of Nova Scotia, according to Mary Theresa. Father MacDonald had kind eyes and a limp because he'd been in a bus crash in Africa when he was there as a missionary. The bus had blown a tire and then they hit a big animal ("Probably an elephant," said Mary Theresa) and rolled into a ravine. Father MacDonald refused to leave until all the other passengers were taken care of; he insisted on saying last rites for the ones who were dying right there on the ground. By the time they got him to the clinic his leg was in a very bad way and it never did heal properly. Father Burke had a jeep.

"It's not his jeep; it belongs to all the priests but none of the others ever drive it," Mary Theresa explained. "Father Cameron and Father MacDonald travel around in that long, shiny black car with the dark windows. The windows are so people can't stare at the nuns when Father MacDonald takes them to the doctor."

Father Burke took boys on weekend camping trips. On the way home from school I'd see the jeep in the church parking lot, doors wide open, and piles of camping gear spread out on the ground. It took hours to load and looked like wonderful fun. Joey went a few times.

"We only ever get to go on Sunday school picnics with our minister." I was envious.

Joey curled his lip. "Father Burke don't take little girls. If he did, you wouldn't want to go. He likes to get the boys alone. You never heard tell of a pervert before?"

Of course I had. I'd seen them. Men in cars who drove along slowly and offered you a ride home. Strangers you didn't talk to. (Not the priest who stood with a hand on Joey's shoulder, talking to Mrs. MacInnes outside their church after Mass. "Yes, Father. No, Father," she said while Joey stared at the ground. Not seeing me when I waved to him and Mary Theresa on my way home from Sunday school.)

The boys in the schoolyard at St. Mike's made jokes.

"You don't want to be a altar boy for Father Burke," they said. "You gets all wore out dodging him."

"Yeah, you wants to keep your back to the wall," and they'd snicker.

"And your catechism down the front of your pants!" and they'd roar with laughter, Joey with them.

I didn't like them laughing. I couldn't see how it was funny.

"Why don't you tell somebody?" I asked Joey, following him down the street.

"Who d'you think they'd believe, you or a priest?"

"But, he's bad."

"Nobody would believe you. You'd get a beating, is all. And then the priest would make it worse for you."

"There must be somebody to tell. There must be something you can do."

We walked in silence. Joey stopped.

"There is." He picked up a rock. "There's this."

It sailed through the air, a long splendid arc, on and down and then, with a wild crystal explosion, shattered the hall window of the Glebe house. The thundering of my blood was the thundering of Joey's feet a block away. A face appeared at the window; a hand turned the doorknob. I bolted, sucking air through my pores.


Tuesday morning there was a patrol car in the schoolyard. Upstairs in the principal's office were two Mounties in yellow-striped pants and scarlet jackets. The priest had seen me running away from the Glebe house; he'd given my description to the RCMP and they were looking for me! They were going to arrest me in front of the whole school and I hadn't done anything! Would they believe me? What could I say to convince them I was innocent without betraying Joey? By the time the bell rang for classes to begin I was close to tears.

All morning the Mounties held interviews. The teachers were edgy and strict. The kids buzzed between the rows; everyone wanted to go to the washroom in hopes of overhearing something good.

Somebody was kidnapped, somebody was murdered, somebody robbed the store on the corner. Everybody had a theory.

By recess it was obvious they were only interviewing boys. It wasn't me they were after. Still, what if they asked about Joey? I wasn't sure I could lie convincingly.

At noon they moved to St. Michael's. We'd eavesdropped on gossiping teachers and the story was coming out, bit by bit. At first I was sure it was another crazy theory. Kids didn't do things like that. Over the weekend some boys had taken a stray dog to the park where we had barbecues and kite-flying contests. They put the dog on one of the spits and lit a fire under it while it was still alive. I threw up in the hall and spent the rest of the afternoon lying on a cot in the teachers' room.

After school, I ran as fast as I could to find Mary Theresa. She was marching along with quick, angry strides. I had a stitch in my side by the time I caught up to her.

"They took Joey." She was furious. "He didn't do it. They took him and three other boys away."

I walked along beside her, wheezing. Joey was good; he saved me from Bruno. The newspaper said he was a hero. "He didn't do it," I said. "Somebody made a mistake. It wasn't him."

Next day, Mary Theresa was defiant. Two boys had been arrested and sent to reform school. Joey and two others had been at the park; they hadn't taken part but had watched and done nothing to stop it. Mary Theresa said the other boys would have killed Joey for sure if he'd opened his mouth. The Mounties knew about the window, too. Old Mrs. Prothero, next door to the Glebe house, had seen him from her upstairs window and told Father Burke. Joey had to report to the Mounties twice a week and he was being sent to a summer camp for troubled boys. He would leave in two weeks when school was finished. Mary Theresa said it was a good place. Joey would learn to hike and canoe and be a better person.

On Grading Day I learned that Father Burke was the director of the camp. It was hot on the sidewalk, a splendid June day. Ice cream was dripping down my elbow; my graduation certificate, my passport to summer, was safe in my hand. Mary Theresa and I, in matching socks and headbands, were strolling home.

"You have to stop him," I told her. "You can't let him go there. Father Burke is bad. He'll hurt Joey." Mary Theresa said nothing. I persisted. "You know what he does. Joey and Mick and Colin told us. He does bad things."

"Shut up!" she screamed. "Shut up, you liar. You dirty Protestant. You friggin' liar. Shut your damn mouth!" She shoved me hard and ran.

The walk home was long and hot and sad. I wished Joey or Mary Theresa or one of the other kids would tell. But when I thought of who I might tell, I couldn't think of anyone either. Not my parents. I hadn't the faintest idea how to approach them with that kind of thing. Our family doctor was cool and remote, my mother's preference. He'd listen to her description of what was wrong with me, look in my ears, or listen to my chest, then write a prescription without ever looking in my face. Our minister? Reverend Paulsen liked church holidays because he could use them as an excuse to wear fancy robes. A closet papist, my father called him, among other things. He would rock up on his tiptoes and wait, smiling, for you to offer him the best seat, the first cup of tea, the last piece of double-chocolate cake. His pulpit voice was rich rolling molasses, and he loved the sound of it. A man who would rather talk than listen.

Who could I tell? No one.

I didn't make up with Mary Theresa. I didn't go to her house. I went to Guide camp and learned to swim. I made popsicle-stick lampshades and pine-cone bookends and learned to recite "Look to This Day" standing around the flagpole before breakfast. I put Joey out of my mind.

When I got back, the end of July, Mary Theresa came over and we hung around the backyard and made lemonade. She invited me to her house and after a few days I went. I played with the babies and we resumed travelling the woods, pretending to look for bootleggers.

Joey came home the last week in August. He was two inches taller, his shoulders were wider, he was tanned and he looked years older. His gaze slid over me as if I were a piece of polished furniture; his eyes were slick as river ice, black as a church coal-bin. I was so

11

uneasy around him that I stopped going to Mary Theresa's house again. I couldn't seem to get my breath when he was in the room. I'd breathe and breathe but the air was a thick fog that wouldn't or couldn't go down into my lungs. My heart beat so fast it made the muscles in my neck and shoulders ache and my ears seemed full of water. I didn't feel much better out in the street. There was an invisible weight balancing on the houses and trees in our neighbourhood, waiting to fall and smother me. I read in the sunporch, played in my bedroom, tried to be quiet and good.

September passed; the murmur of classrooms and shrieks of the schoolyards gave me comfort. Each morning that I woke to find the world unchanged and ordinary, the weight lifted a little more. Then it was almost Hallowe'en and I was obsessed, along with Mary Theresa, with designing and assembling our costumes.

Hallowe'en night we ran, walked, trudged for miles, gathering as much booty as possible before our curfew. By ten-thirty we were sorting on the dining-room table: a bag of chips for Thursday, a chocolate bar for Friday, double treats for Saturday. We did this every year and every year we nibbled our schedule to pieces in less than a week.

"Make yourselves sick and be done with it," Mother said.

My brother burst into the kitchen, flung his candy on the counter. "The Glebe house is on fire!" and he was gone.

"Stay here." Mother snatched her sweater and ran. When she disappeared around the corner we hared out the back way and took the shortcut to St. Mike's.

Smoke billowed from the windows; flames licked up the shingles. The street was a carnival of trucks, firemen, fountains of water, spinning lights and a crowd of witches, ghosts, monsters and tramps, their collars clutched by mothers in cardigans and slippers.

Joey was part of a line of men and older boys keeping back the curious, the foolishly reckless.

"Get on home," he ordered Mary Theresa and me. "It's too dangerous. Sparks is flying everywhere." His voice was solemn but wonderfully elated, like the minister's on Easter morning. He looked directly at me for the first time in months. Flames flickered and leapt in his eyes, waving finger-lights that coaxed and threatened.

"Do as I tell you," he said gently. "Go home before you get hurt."

I fell back, my mouth full of secrets, my jaw clenched tight to keep them from spilling out into the chilly night air. I yanked at her arm but Mary Theresa wouldn't budge so I left without her. The streets were quiet, the houses empty; everyone was at the fire. I ate my Thursday treat, my Friday treat. I ate Saturday's double treat, a Mars bar and a bag of chips. I was beginning to feel a little queasy so I started in on Sunday's licorice whips, and chewy Hallowe'en kisses in their orange-and-black wrappers with hissing cats and ugly crones. I ate through to the middle of November and then I threw it all up.

Mother found me in the bathroom on my knees, vomit all down my front, the toilet bowl floating half-chewed chips and candy in a murky chocolate soup. I was crying.

"What a goose," she said to my father. "When I told her to make herself sick and be done with it I never dreamed she'd actually do it."

She told everyone. When Mrs. MacInnes phoned at midnight to ask if Mary Theresa was there, Mother told.

"She's such a literal child," she said. "She takes everything so seriously. You have to watch every word you say to her."

# Butterflies at Le Chat d'Or

"This baby could take us all the way to Vancouver," said Donna's father, polishing the side-view mirror with his handkerchief. "Hell, it could take us to California!"

"Quebec," said her mother. "We're going to Quebec."

"I know that." He took two suitcases from her and stacked them in the trunk. "I'm just saying it's one solid car. We could cruise on down to Mexico in this car."

"Two weeks in Quebec, then home again. I want this car to last."

"I'm just saying."

Donna closed the door on their bickering, leaned back on the sun-warmed leather and took a deep breath. The car, a '61 Chevy, was almost new and the first one her mother trusted to transport the family long-distance. There were no food smells, no baby puke, no odour of stale cigarettes—just leather, pine air freshener and adventure. Me and Dad could go to Mexico, thought Donna. We could leave Mom and the baby in Ste-Anne with Grandma and keep right on going. Stay in hotels with swimming pools like the Cleverleigh Inn out on Highway 57.

But by day two her dad was snarly because a short somewhere had blown out half the gauges, her mom had stubbed a pack of du

Mauriers into the ashtray, and Cathy, the baby, had thrown up twice—once by the side of the road and once, because they hadn't stopped soon enough, on Donna's new pink sandals. At night they camped in a cavernous army-surplus tent that took a lot of yelling and sweating and snivelling to raise.

By the time she was thirteen, and old enough to be mortified by ancient green canvas, her mother'd put her foot down and bought a water-repellent, nylon six-sleeper from Canadian Tire. Once the tent was up, a much simpler procedure, Donna strolled the camp-grounds, checking out other families. Cute guys who camped with their parents, she discovered, were few and far between and too often carried small editions of the New Testament in their shirt pockets. Not quite what she was praying for.

It always rained in New Brunswick and when it thinned to a drizzle mosquitoes as big as fruit bats rose from the grass and fol-lowed her to little log-house washrooms, back to the tent and into her plaid-lined sleeping bag. She sprayed Muskol in her hair so she could sleep in peace.

By the time they hit Rivière-du-Loup she and Cathy were not speaking to each other and usually had been fined a week's allowance for squabbling while their father was trying to think. Cathy sprawled a knee or elbow marginally over on Donna's side, scratching mosquito bites until blood ran down her legs and dripped too close to Donna. Donna fought the urge to slap her. Past Rivière-du-Loup, the air seemed brighter. Cathy moved back to her own side and sat up to look out her window. The long slide down the St. Lawrence was better; there was the river with hills and farms on the other side, and small grocery stores where they watched their mother struggle in rusty French to buy milk and hot dogs. Close to the city they weren't allowed to talk because their father was a nervous wreck. He kept one foot poised above the brake, one above the gas, jerking to a halt, then bouncing forward through the traffic.

"Christly maniacs," he muttered as he was edged into the wrong lane, again.

"According to the map . . . ," her mother began.

"The map's a piece of crap." He wiped his forehead with a wad of tissues from the box on the seat between them. "That's a red light, buddy!" he yelled out the window. "Red! Or are you blind as well as stupid?" Her father never yelled.

Her mother folded the map, folded her hands, and gazed out the opposite window. Cathy sucked quietly on her blanket. Donna clutched the seat behind her father and tried not to breathe on him. After miles of apartment buildings fronted with iron balconies and curving stairs peopled with families sitting out, reading newspapers, drinking, talking, snoozing, and once a man in an undershirt playing a fiddle, they were finally on the right street, in the right lane for the bridges.

That first summer Donna had been terrified. Had never seen so high or so long a bridge. Cars sped past in the outside lane as her father cursed and their tires roared on the metal bed. She knew in her belly there were too many cars and their weight would crack the bridge. Butterflies clung to her insides and clenched their eyes. She took feather breaths: the volume of air in her lungs was crucial; one greedy lungful might snap the steel beneath them. The roadway would fall down and the two ends swing away from each other, curving back to the shore and shaking cars into the St. Lawrence like pepper into soup. Finally she could see the end, and cars safe again on the other side. If she didn't move or blink . . .

When they reached land Donna's eyeballs felt as if they'd been rolled in hot sand. Then—another bridge. She sat straight, took precisely spaced breathlets, grappled the north shore with her gaze and reeled it in. The huge cross on the hill lit up; they were still alive and would be at Grandma's soon.


Her grandma and her three aunts lived with their families in a row of white-painted houses on a blacktopped country road surrounded by hayfields and sandy gullies full of chokecherry bushes and bronze grackles. The uncles worked in St-Jérôme or Montreal and the little cousins ran around sunburnt, playing endless games of Let's Pretend.

Donna slept at her Aunt Bea's with her cousin Sharon. Her parents stayed with Aunt Lillian and Grandma. When Cathy was old enough she stayed with Aunt Linnet and Uncle Charles because she was the same age as their Rosemary. Rosemary's older sister, Peggy, was Sharon's age, a year older than Donna. The Unholy Trio, Uncle Charles called them. Mornings they stayed in Sharon's room backcombing each other's hair and painting their nails while the aunts visited each other's kitchens, drank coffee and said, "I don't think I can take it much longer," to which the others would reply, "What about the kids?" and "What will you do for money?"

Donna stopped fretting about this kind of talk after a certain amount of repetition, although the year she was fifteen and they came by train without her father Peggy tried to make something of it.

"My father had a girlfriend," she announced. Donna was shocked; she liked Uncle Charles. "When she started calling the house, Mama told her she'd whip her ass from here to Val-d'Or if she didn't leave Daddy alone. Then she told Daddy to get the hell out; Dominic Aucoin was back from Labrador and he still had all his hair. Scared Daddy so much he hasn't been out after dark since."

"My father does not have a girlfriend." Donna twisted the lid of her bottle of Midnight Mauve enamel so tightly she stripped the thread and cracked the plastic. "Shit," she said.

"Take it easy," said Sharon. "It's not the end of the friggin' world."

"It's not anything," said Donna. "It's bullshit is what it is."

Peggy rolled her eyes and leaned into the mirror to check her mascara for clumps. "The children are always the last to know."


"I want you to spend an hour a day with your grandmother," her mother insisted.

"Doing what? I don't know what to say to her."

"It doesn't matter. She's an old woman and she only sees you a few weeks a year. Ask about her life. Tell her about yours."

"I have no life."

"Don't be smart. Tell her about school." Her mother bragged up Donna's marks to the aunts, who then held her up as an example to her cousins. Sharon offered to lend her a set of falsies she'd worn when she was twelve.

"You don't have boobs because you study too much," she explained. "All your body energy goes to your head." Sharon wore a C cup and almost never studied.

"Forget it!" said Donna's mother when Sharon pranced about in a pair of tight red pedal-pushers and a black scooped T-shirt. "Bea is out of her mind. I'd shoot you before I'd let you walk around dressed like that."

Her mother thought Aunt Bea was slack with her kids and that Sharon was a bad influence on Donna, but she wasn't going to start an argument with Bea and upset Grandma; she hissed orders at Donna instead.

It was always hot; everything was limp by ten o'clock: hair, clothes, chickens in the yard, dogs under the porches. After lunch the aunts napped and the older girls took the little kids north of the houses to play in a shallow stream. Water rambled brown and sandy over a wide bottom; chokecherry branches dipped into the flow. Their wine-red berries filled Donna's mouth with wool. Leo, who was six, pulled off his clothes and kicked up spray. The little girls moved upstream, pelting him with clots of wet sand when he tried to follow.

"Little cannibal," Cathy spat.

"You mean savage," said Rosemary. "Cannibals eats people; savages is naked."

"They won't play with me," Leo whined to Peggy.

"Well, what do you expect," she told him, "running around naked, like a little heathen. Put your pants back on and go play with the boys." She sent him downstream where the others were building a dam with sticks and rocks, hoping to make the water deep enough for swimming.

"He'll just mess it up," they complained.

"You let him play, or we're all going back to the house!"

Sharon stretched out in the sun, oiled, with a paper tent on her nose. "One of you watch them kids. You can drown in three inches of water, you know."

Peggy smoked, facing away from the stream so the kids couldn't see and tell on her. Donna opened *Mist on the Heather* to page sixty-four. Sharon had a boxful of books under her bed—trash, Donna's mother said, but she read them herself in the sunporch when she thought Donna wasn't around. All the aunts read romance novels. Brett, the heroine, had just been rescued from a mudslide by the local laird who, until now, had treated her with contempt but was unaccountably, tenderly, pouring her toddies by his blazing hearth. Donna's oily fingers smudged the pages; she was squirmy and hollow-bellied in the heat. The toddies made Brett drowsy. "Stay awake," muttered Donna, but no luck, so the laird's housekeeper put Brett to bed. *Merde*, thought Donna, who couldn't swear properly in French although her cousins coached her regularly. *Merde* she understood, but how, in particular, could religious artifacts having nothing to do with sex be swear words? When she said *calice* it sounded stupid and ineffectual. Maybe they were fooling her; maybe they were lying. She couldn't exactly consult her mother. She closed her eyes and made up a different ending: French kissing and some butterfly-dance groping before the virginal Brett called a reluctant, sticky halt.

The payoff for babysitting in the afternoons, besides cash, was permission to go to Le Chat d'Or after supper. Two miles down the blacktop, pushing, teasing and perfecting their lipstick in mirrored compacts. Le Chat d'Or was part of a grocery store. M. Gautier sat on a stool in a cave at the front. On the counter was a brass register with worn keys and a smooth-scooped coin tray. In behind were cigarettes, girlie magazines and, according to rumour, bootleg booze. When he had to cut baloney or cheese for a customer M. Gautier locked the cash, lifted up a section of the counter and swung down to the cooler at the back. He lifted the hems of women's skirts with his crutches, his idea of a joke.

"I'd break his crutch over his cruddy head. Old goat," said Sharon. But he left her and her friends alone, preferring to torment middle-aged women who were too flustered to yell at a cripple.

His nephew had renovated a storeroom and the result was Le Chat d'Or: green-and-yellow-flowered linoleum, yellow plywood walls, four booths with the same flowered linoleum on the tabletops, an old jukebox against the back wall. They drank Pepsi, jived with each other and waited for their friends to show up. This is Jacques, they'd say, this is Serge. The boys slow-danced with Peggy and Sharon, ran their hands up and down their backs, whispered into their ears. When Jacques' or Serge's hand rounded a curve of buttock, a loud thumping would shake the wall between Le Chat d'Or and the store, pounding until all hands were back where they belonged.

"He has a spy hole," the cousins said. "He watches us all the time. Hopes he'll see something. *Cochon.*"

The boys didn't dance with Donna. She sat and smiled and got bloated from too much Pepsi. She wanted to be witty and cute, to charm them, but doubted they'd care that "la plume de ma tante est sur le bureau." Her cousins were failing French at school; they couldn't spell and their grammar was a joke, unlike Donna who made nineties in her P.E.I. classroom. Her cousins were dancing and making naughty French puns; she was not. She didn't want hands all over her body—at least she was pretty sure she didn't—but she did want to be asked to dance; she did want some of that smoky, heated attention.

She ran her finger through the condensation, tipped the bottle back and took a swig, letting in enough air so it wouldn't make a sucking noise when she stopped.

"Smoke?" offered Peggy, pulling one out of Serge's pack.

"My mother'd kill me."

"You are a baby," said Sharon. "Here, watch." She flipped her bangs out of her eyes and inhaled. "Slow, like this." Placed it between Donna's lips where it dangled until she got a grip on it. She inhaled, just a little, held the smoke in her mouth, blew it out.

"You have to get it into your lungs to get the good of it. Try again."

Donna choked, tried again.

"Better. I smoked half a dozen before I did it that good."

Donna steadied her throat muscles, drew a little deeper, admiring the fit of the long butt in her fingers. Sharon took it from her, blew a smoke ring, then mashed it out.

"Help yourself." She flipped Jacques' pack onto the table and pulled him back to dance. When they took a break and scrunched into the booth he laid an arm behind Sharon's head and pulled her close to neck, his fingers fanned across her throat. Donna watched through her eyelashes. She lit another cigarette. Sharon and Jacques didn't seem to need to breathe. There must be a trick to it, thought Donna, like letting air in the side of the Pepsi bottle.

"When's Dad coming?" she asked her mother.

"I don't know. Where's Cathy? Aunt Linnet needs you both to pick currants."

The cousins were ripping trusses of red fruit from the bushes and throwing them at the bowl. "I hate these things," said Sharon. "I don't even like currant jelly."

"Serge's mother makes currant wine, but she counts every bottle so he doesn't think he can sneak one."

"Never mind. Jacques' cousin will get us some beer." Beer to celebrate the end of July, Peggy and Serge's six-month anniversary, and Donna's upcoming birthday. Sharon had a purse full of breath mints and anyway Donna only planned to take a sip to see what it was like.

The afternoon went on forever. The little kids were bored and quarrelsome. Cathy got stung by a wasp and yelled as if her arm were coming off. Brett went dancing with the laird's ne'er-do-well cousin in a blue taffeta dress with violets in her golden hair. Donna had straight, won't-show-the-dirt brown hair, like Sharon's would have been if Aunt Bea hadn't let her frost it (Sharon's father never even knew the difference). The ne'er-do-well cousin behaved in a most ungentlemanly fashion and ripped the front of the blue taffeta dress. The laird rescued Brett and pressed a violet into his breast pocket.

Finally they were free to go. They met behind the elementary school, screened by the brick walls and rusty swings. Donna's butterflies jived and twisted. Jacques and Serge were late; they'd already drunk some of the beer. She was introduced to Marie-Claire and Georges. Marie-Claire used to be Jacques' girlfriend but when he forgot her birthday she broke up with him. Before she was ready to forgive him Sharon snapped him up, so Sharon and Marie-Claire weren't best friends anymore. The beer was warm. Beaver pee must taste like this, thought Donna. Georges took the bottle she was nursing and finished it in one swallow.

"Georges has his brother's car so we're going to a dance in St-Jérôme. It'll be great." Sharon waved her bottle at Donna.

"But we have to be home in an hour. There isn't time."

"So we'll be late. We'll tell them we had a flat tire."

"But I don't have permission to go to a dance."

Peggy and Sharon coaxed and threatened. If she went home alone they'd catch shit. She wouldn't sit in the schoolyard in the dark until they came back, either. Finally they followed her home, so pissed off they couldn't think of names bad enough to call her. Donna was cross too, mostly because she knew damn well if they'd gone, Jacques would slow-dance all night with Sharon, Marie-Claire would settle for Georges, Peggy would have Serge, and she would be the gooseberry again. She was sick of it. She was the visitor, she was the guest—they could have invited a boy for her. If they'd any manners. If they weren't so selfish.

When they got home, her mother had gone for a long drive with her father, who had arrived after driving day and night from P.E.I.

"He barely said hello," Cathy complained. "I showed him my wasp sting and Mom said don't bother him. Then they left. I'm not going to sleep until they come back."

"Move over." Donna did not want to share a bed with Sharon.

"Only if you read me a story."

So she read *Mist on the Heather* until Cathy fell asleep, then turned out the lamp and watched passing headlights swing from wall to wall. None turned into her grandma's driveway.

Peggy woke them in the morning, wailing and pounding on the sheets. "Get up, get up. They're dead."

"They" was Georges. Too drunk to make the turn onto the

Ste-Croix bridge, he'd clipped a girder and spun the car through the railing. Jacques had a smashed arm and a ruptured spleen, Serge had cuts and bruises, and Marie-Claire, who'd been in front, in the death seat, had head injuries.

"They don't know if she's going to make it," sobbed Sharon. "They had to operate on Jacques. Daddy's taking me to the hospital at lunchtime."

Peggy went with her but Donna stayed home to keep an eye on her parents. Her mother sat in Grandma's kitchen with the aunts; they thanked their lucky stars their daughters knew better than to get in a car with a boy who'd been drinking.

"That poor girl's parents," they said. "I suppose she never gave them a thought."

"She was terrible boy-crazy," said Linnet, shaking her head. She's dying, thought Donna, trying to pour herself a cup of coffee and spilling it on her hand. And Georges is dead. What did it matter if Marie-Claire was boy-crazy? Why did they talk as if she deserved what she'd got? Donna wiped up the spill and pushed past them to the door, then slammed it behind her. The little girls were playing with paper dolls on the steps, pebbles holding the clothes down in tiered rows. She scattered tabbed dresses and playsuits and ran from Rosemary and Cathy's outraged screeches. "Fat pig!" "Snot-faced meanie!" they called.

She slipped between the tangle of pin-cherry branches and the back wall of the house. Peeling green, where the rest of the house was white, because Uncle Stan couldn't be bothered painting the side no one saw. The foundation stones were covered in moss and the ground was sour and rocky. No one ever went there, because there were snakes. Donna hoped she'd see one so she could throw rocks at it. When the car started to skid, what had Marie-Claire thought? And Georges? One mistake, and everything is taken from you. It could have been me, thought Donna, or Sharon, or Peggy. They'd come home because she was jealous, not because she was good, or thinking of her parents. She hated her aunts and her mother. Couldn't stand the smugness in their voices. She almost told them who-all was boy-crazy and who was very nearly dead. She'd have gone with her cousins in a minute if there'd been a boy for her; they'd all have been wrapped around that bridge if she hadn't made them come home.

Her father got up, had lunch, then went and gassed up the car while her mother packed. They left for P.E.I. at three in the afternoon, her mother driving while her father slept.

Donna had her birthday in New Brunswick, turned sixteen and nobody noticed. Later they made up for it: in September she got her beginner's licence, and her mother let her frost her hair. "Don't tell your father," she said.

The next summer they stopped for two days in Ste-Anne on their way to Prince George, B.C., where her dad had a new job. Le Chat d'Or had burned down the previous winter.

"For the insurance," suggested Peggy. Sharon's new boyfriend had his own car and he offered to take the three cousins to visit Marie-Claire, but there wasn't enough time. Donna didn't really want to go anyway, no matter how pretty the grounds, how friendly the nuns. The next year her grandmother died and it was too far to travel so they never went to Ste-Anne for vacations again.

\* \* \*

Peggy is late.

"She's always late." Sharon shakes out a pair of tiny reading glasses and scans the menu. "Perrier with a twist," she tells the waiter. Her hair is cropped, a honey blond. She's wearing a red silk suit and chunks of gold. She weighs seven pounds less than she did at sixteen.

"You've been studying the market too much," teases Donna. "Your boobs are shrinking." She hasn't seen the cousins in almost four years, not since Linnet's funeral.

Sharon is flashing pictures of her three granddaughters.

"She loves it that people think they're her kids," says Peggy, who arrives carrying her uniform in a dry-cleaning bag; she goes on shift in two hours. "That's why she carries five hundred snapshots of them in her purse."

Sharon's son, Guy, was born when she was eighteen.

"I'm never doing that again," she'd said and harassed a doctor in Ontario until he agreed to tie her tubes. She's been selling real estate since her twenties and she's good at it. "Every time Quebec tries to separate I make a little money. Sell, buy—either way I get my percentage."

"She's a ghoul," says Peggy, fishing out her own pictures. Her sixth child is almost two. "Everyone thinks I'm crazy," she'd written Donna, "but I love having babies and I'm not ready to be old so here I go again." René, in red OshKosh overalls, stares down the camera with his enormous chocolate eyes.

"So gorgeous," confides Sharon, "you could eat him with a spoon."

Donna's two are teenagers. She lives in mortal fear they'll get up to some of the stuff she did. End up like Marie-Claire, twenty years in a wheelchair, unable to speak.

"She still loved the Beach Boys, though," says Sharon, who had visited her every month, set her hair and painted her nails, until she died of pneumonia. Sharon leans over to light Peggy's cigarette. Neither smokes. Unless it's a special occasion. Donna quit ten years ago herself, after her divorce. At one time or another they've all been through a divorce.

"How are you doing for money?" they'd asked. "Are the kids all right?"

They disagree on damn near everything, but ten minutes in their presence and Donna wants to shake off her shoes, put her elbows on the table and light up. She's given up trying to figure it, or them, out. If they weren't my cousins, she thinks, I'd never be friends with these women.

"Give me one of those," she says.

# *Ceely's Choice*

Ceely reached through darkness. Her fingers touched the clock face, then slid up to switch off the alarm ten minutes before it was due to ring. She pushed the covers aside, sat up on the edge of her bed and waited for details to emerge: the carved footboard, the glass knobs on the dresser, the grey rectangle of lace at the window. When everything was in place she pulled on her robe, tied it tightly and slippered her way down the back stairs to the kitchen where she rattled up the wood stove for a little heat and began to make breakfast. Porridge, toast, eggs, bacon, tea. Pack the lunches, fill the Thermos bottles. When everything was ready, she called them down: Elias, George, and Thomas James.

They ate without conversation, nodding and grunting for her to refill their cups. Thick and burly with the same wheat-stubble jaw and gingery eyes, they appeared to be one person at different stages of his life. Thomas James was twenty-nine, Elias fifty-one, George, named for his father, forty. As soon as they were out the door she cleared the table, washed the dishes and, taking ten minutes for herself, sat in her rocker by the porch window to watch the sun climb over the fields and paint in the colours of her flower beds.

By noon she had cleaned the house, canned eight quarts of

beans, made bread, biscuits, pies (two raspberry, two blueberry) and prepared the midday meal. They were late returning; it was Saturday and the gear had to be well baited for the weekend. They dropped their clothes—wet and smelling of rotten herring—in the porch and washed up in the pantry before sitting down to dinner. Their talk was all of fishing: prices, catches, thieves, wars out on the grounds, crooked buyers, money made and lost. Ceely poured tea, served pie, cleaned up. One by one the boys headed upstairs to nap.

The house was so still she could hear a beetle clicking among the logs in the woodbox. The clock in the hall ticked, paused as a gentle rest note fell between each second. She felt she lived two lives, one the tick of time, the other the silence between. In the silence between she went into the back parlour, cool without a south window to let in the summer sun. Across the backs of two sawhorses lay the quilting frame her grandfather had made for her grandmother as a courting gift more than a century before, both their initials carved on one of the long hardwood boards. It was one of the few things Ceely had brought when she'd married into this family—the frame, some clothing, an autoharp and a new wringer washer. The washer had gone to the dump after thirty years of hard use; the autoharp was somewhere in the attic, long since broken by furiously quarrelling children.

Ceely had been taught to quilt by her grandmother, Elizabeth, stitching small scraps of fabric together, pricking her fingers over and over, ripping out the stitches and trying again. By her eighth birthday she had completed her first top. Together they put the backing, batt and top onto the frame and when it was tight and even they quilted the layers together. It had been difficult to find a thimble small enough for Ceely. She began with the smallest possible size, heavily padded inside with cotton so it wouldn't fall off. It was uncomfortable and it made her finger sweat but Elizabeth had insisted she wear it.

Each winter they quilted; they made traditional pieced designs, usually with biblical overtones: Jacob's Ladder, King David's Crown, Robbing Peter to Pay Paul. Then, when Ceely was almost seventeen, Elizabeth had a heart attack and died. Ceely was orphaned for a second time.

They'd been making currant jelly out in the summer kitchen. Sweat ran down their faces, armpits, spines, pooled in the backs of their knees and between their buttocks. The flies, swarming the window screens, were wild to get at the sweet bubblings. Elizabeth sat down on a straight-backed chair to rest, fly swatter at the ready. Nothing offended her more than the sight of two flies noisily, madly engaging in intercourse. They would do it on your food, on your leg, on the sticky wooden spoon resting on a chipped saucer. She leaned over and smashed them with the swatter, then continued forward until she hit the stove. The jam pot skittered off and crashed against the back wall. She slid to the floor and the swatter fell from her hand; an inspired throng of flies scraped through cracks in the window frames and flung themselves at the sticky spatters.

The neighbours took charge and Ceely—her modest inheritance lost to back taxes and bank loans—was married into a family from across the river: to run and fetch for her mother-in-law, to serve and clean up after her father-in-law, to lie quiet and compliant for her husband.

After the old people died and her children were mostly grown, Ceely brought her quilting frame down from the attic and set it up in a quiet spot. There, she began again. Intricately pieced, vibrantly coloured, the quilts were her winter gardens. At first they were pieced from the scraps and remnants she had on hand, later from lengths of fabric bought in town. Still later she searched out specific shades in fabric stores in three counties, or dyed pieces of cloth herself if they were not to be found. She chose patterns because their names appealed to her: Stepping Stones, Flying Geese. She entered The Rocky Road to Kansas in the agricultural exhibition and won first prize. She won again with The Wheel of Chance, Winding Ways and The Delectable Mountains. Something about the oblique slant of her scissors, a twist in her interpretation of these traditional patterns caught the eye. Her colours seemed to explode from the centre, tumbling over one another in a rush for freedom. Only the firm dark borders she placed around the edges kept the colours from flinging themselves off the quilt altogether. She tried her hand at appliqué; she couldn't draw a simple petal shape on paper but she could take scissors and cloth and snip out entire scenes: extravagant gardens, magical forests. You felt you could step into her quilts. You longed to step into her quilts.

In the bottom drawer of the dining-room buffet lay prize ribbon after ribbon, and every bed in the house had at least three quilts. A few special favourites were carefully folded in the hall chest. She had begun sending some to her daughter Beth, who lived in Ottawa, first as presents, later to keep them safe. It made her ill to see the stains, the cigarette burns, the careless rips in her handiwork.

"You must think of selling some," Beth wrote. "I'm running out of storage space and it's a pity to pack them away unappreciated. I swear I've enough for an exhibit! Come for a long visit and I'll ask Marion to mount a show in her gallery. People will love them. You could have some real money of your own. The boys won't starve. Get out the can opener and give them a crash course in how to use it."

Ceely dismissed the idea as foolish; she didn't take it seriously, but sometimes, sitting at the frame, she imagined a long cool room with polished floors and ivory walls. Her quilts stretched off into the distance, a river of colour. From somewhere came delicate music, flutes or violins; she eavesdropped on the admiring comments of strangers.

In and out, her silver needle was a minnow skimming a roil of green prints and plains. The pattern was a variation of The Storm at Sea, an old favourite and so familiar she could stitch eleven to the inch and set her mind free to roam her imaginary gallery. She was almost finished; another hour would have it off the frame. Something in it was skewed: it began quietly at the centre but the movement of a curve, the out-of-plumb push of the triangles built foaming green-glass waves that smashed outwards in all directions; the storm became a hurricane. Ceely's Choice, she called it for now. Once she'd labelled them Variations on _____; now all her quilts were Ceely's Choice until their true names came to her.

Her husband once sold one of her quilts. He pulled it off the clothesline and took it to a tavern where he got thirty dollars for it. He used the money to buy rum and came home drunk and belligerent. She didn't speak to him or look at him for weeks. He hardly seemed to notice but he didn't do it again. When he died, she put her first Wedding Ring quilt in the bottom of the coffin to ease his rest. He'd stopped knocking her about the last few years of his life and his temper had thinned to an ineffectual trickle. For a little while she missed him.

From upstairs came the muffled thump of sock feet on the floor. She pulled off her thimble, tucked it into her apron pocket and closed the door on Ceely's Choice.

While the boys were out doing chores she did a few loads of wash to hang on the outside line. Supper was cold ham and potato salad. More pie. They began drinking immediately after supper and within an hour had opened a second forty-ouncer. Ceely washed the dishes as they pulled out the cards and got down to it. Three of their friends came by with more rum. Her head began to throb with the smoke and the noise.

"Have a drink, Ma," roared Thomas James. "It'll do you good, for Christ's sake. Put a smile on that jeezlus sour face of yours!"

She tried to pull up the corners of her mouth but her lips were as stiff as week-old dirty socks. She went out to wander in her flower beds, weeding among the dahlias, picking off the spent pansy blooms, crushing the leaves of the lemon verbena between her palms to release their soothing fragrance.

By ten-thirty Malcolm had gone home to his wife, Neal and Bobbie to Westvale to a dance. The boys never went to dances, nor were they likely to marry unless, of course, she died and they needed a housekeeper. They continued to play and drink for several hours more until finally they staggered upstairs, Elias leaning on a bottle.

She opened the windows to air the kitchen. Her headache eased slightly but she didn't feel able to sleep quite yet. She went back to the parlour and in the lamplight finished the last border. The smell of smoke still lingered, drifted through the gap between door top and frame, floated above her head.

Her mind paused, stalled. The roar had moved from her head to the rooms above; the smoke was fresh and curling about the moulding. The door handle was cool; the hall beyond was clear but for a foot of smoke obscuring the ceiling. Flames licked down the wallpaper in the stairwell, reached along the banister towards her. She stood, frozen, until a voice began to direct her. Elizabeth's voice, as cool and composed as the lavender-scented gloves she had worn to church.

Ceely stepped back into the room, ripped out the basting threads that held the quilt to the frame, then folded it and laid it over her arm. She turned right along the front hall and, bending beneath the quickly lowering pall, opened the chest. She lifted free a prize-winning Dresden Plate and her beloved Grandmother's Choice, pieced from her own wedding dress, Elizabeth's favourite summer print and Beth's christening gown. Then she stepped out the front door and closed it behind her.

The moon had risen over the black trees at the lawn's edge. Wet grass licked at her ankles. She ran a finger over the design of her Grandmother's Choice, tracing the curves and edges. The moon bleached and silvered the colours but in her mind's eye she could see the faded lilac and rose of Elizabeth's dress. She'd worn it to church often and it reminded Ceely of cool dark pews, echoing coughs and whispers, and the sound of a pump organ. The sprigged blue muslin had been her wedding dress, and mediating between the two fabrics were strips cut from Beth's christening gown of white lawn. Ceely had wanted to include its lace trim but it was too decorative and made the piece seem trivial and pretty so she'd left it off. The quilt was unlike her usual vibrant landscapes or freewheeling carnivals. She'd made it not to be exhibited for prizes, not to be hung in a gallery, but to lie in a worn and polished wooden chest, to be pulled up over her shoulders on a cold night, to flap and billow on the line outside her pantry window. It looked as though it had been made a long, long time ago, loved and aged with gentle use.

From behind came riffs of spit and crackle, the deep roar of hot winds and the percussion of imploding glass, but she did not turn to look. Her shoulders began to ache slightly with the weight of the quilts but she would not abandon them; instead she hugged them closer to her chest and began the long walk across the fields to wake the neighbours.

# Listening and Touching

My thighs stuck to the chair seat and made sucking noises when I moved. The dress was too damn short but it was all I'd been able to find in Linda's closet. I tried to force the skirt in the direction of my knees as I held my mouth steady in a pleasant smile. I wanted to stay in the city for the summer; I needed this job. The owner of MacCurdy's Fine Fabrics skimmed my application, eyes icing up behind his half-moon glasses as he read "Art School." He thawed slightly when I burbled on about my studies in costume design and how I'd always loved to sew. Perhaps he was feeling reckless; maybe he just liked the dress. He sent me downtown to be trained in his bargain store.

Louise, the manager, was five foot nothing and skinny and could heft a forty-pound bolt of fabric up to her shoulder and heave it onto a shelf overhead. She had lacquered mahogany hair and scurried about in a navy blue smock and size-three flats. Calf-strain and collapsed arches had forced her to give up high heels. She kept them all, though, twenty-seven pairs of pointy-toed four-inchers; twenty-seven different shades lined up on shelves in her bedroom closet. One pair had lucite heels embedded with sunbursts.

"My New Year's Eve shoes. I won't tell you what I paid for them."

MacCurdy trusted Louise. She'd worked for him since 1952. Her husband had died six months after their wedding. He'd worked at the shipyard—a good job until a snapped cable cut him in two. She lost the baby; she went to work. "Life's a crapshoot." She slammed another bolt overhead. "You make your way the best you can."

The store was an alleyway with a glass front, mouldy carpeting, a tiny washroom, an office/lunchroom two people could almost squeeze into, and bolts and bolts of fabric stacked on plywood shelves. Few of the high-priced silks, cut velvets or Victory cottons made it to this store. We were there to sell polyester knit, sixty inches wide, in every imaginable synthetic colour: poisonous pink, acid green, sycophantic baby blue. The bolts were seconds or thirds with splotches where the dye hadn't taken and most had flaws running down the centre. Older ladies in worn leather pumps bought skirt lengths; younger women in plastic slingbacks bought patterns for jumpsuits and enough yardage to run them up. According to Louise, the profit was in the Russians.

Some of them must have been Poles or Rumanians or some other nationality but this was the seventies and they all flew the hammer and sickle from the mast and they all sounded alike to me. Cruising downtown in small groups, dressed in black, they carried plastic suitcases and fur hats. Even in the summer they carried those hats, black, brown or grey, silver- or copper-tipped. They tucked them under their arms while they examined fabrics, tested weights between thumb and forefinger. They would tap me on the arm and point, ask "How much?" or shrug questioningly, and when I told them three or four or five, holding up the correct number of fingers to make the amount clear, they would hold up so many fingers of their own to indicate the number of yards to cut. Or just hand me a bolt and watch as I rolled it out.

"Da," they would say and point to where I should cut, make snipping motions with nicotine-blackened fingers. I'd cut, fold and bag, then figure the total on scrap paper. Meanwhile they would have their money out, Canadian bills with many creases.

Speculators, I thought. They would resell the horrid stuff, women in babushkas paying double and more for something purple and Canadian, something scarlet and foreign. I didn't like these men; they frightened me. Their voices were harsh and they sounded angry.

One morning, one Russian turned his head to speak to a friend, and under his beard, from ear to Adam's apple, was a long pink scar. An inch wide, eight inches long, crumpled and shiny like satin binding dropped on the floor. I pulled my eyes away and rolled out fabric, jerking the bolt, yank, thump, thud. Someone had cut his throat. How had he survived? When someone cuts your throat, you die. My brother, Allister, told me so when I was seven. Once the big artery is cut there's no stopping the bleeding.

"Like this." He pulled back my head and scraped his fingernail across my throat. I screamed, he laughed. "You couldn't scream if I cut it; all's you could do is gurgle. It'd be over in minutes." What kind of sound would come from a cut throat? Vowels, clotted with terror.

I called Louise, handed her the scissors and went to the bathroom and locked the door. I smoked two cigarettes, read a magazine and, when I thought he'd gone, came back out.

"Did you see that?" asked Louise. "Him with the scar across his throat? Some gruesome!"

"No."

"They bought thirty yards so I gave them an extra half yard. They were buying for their mothers," Louise joked.

I wouldn't give them extra fabric, although we had a certain latitude, a few inches per yard. But sometimes there would be a younger one, a boy, scatter-haired and bashful. Maybe with one of the girls who gutted fish on the offshore factory ship. A girl in a printed scarf and rubber boots. Those boys bought fabric for love, I was sure. Romance, lust—fleeting or otherwise, it didn't matter to me. I'd cut an extravagant length and bundle it up quickly, my eye on Louise. I wanted to whisper, "Don't buy this crap. Look there, watered silk, blue as the North Atlantic. Buy it for her, give her something wonderful. It says ten dollars a yard but buy one and I'll cut you two and a half. Do you know what the markup is? Three hundred, five hundred percent." But I didn't speak Russian, and maybe she wouldn't have wanted blue silk anyway. I wondered how they managed love talk in Russian. The language sounded so hard, all edges and exclamations, rigid gutterals and serrated consonants. How could you soften those sounds for the bedroom?

My brother brought home a classmate from navigation school one Thanksgiving when I was still in high school. He was from Belize, Robert Something-or-other. He had such a lilt in his voice; I'd never heard a sound like that come out of a man's mouth. Slow music, it softened all my joints. I asked him questions all weekend just to keep him talking.

My first year of college I took up with Ian, from up past Inverness. I was walking through the cafeteria, a week into the fall term, when I heard him speak. I stopped and sat down beside him. Something Celtic about his *s*'s, the way he pushed them soft and sweet through his teeth, the vowels stretched out and lush. I wanted to get tangled up in those sounds, that tongue, those teeth. That's pretty much how it went all winter. He'd open his mouth, begin to talk, and I'd have to be wherever he was. He moved in with Linda and me after a while. She didn't mind; he paid his share.

After four weeks MacCurdy shifted me to the big store uptown. The main store was closer to my apartment; I could sleep an extra half-hour and still walk to work.

The salesladies in twin sets, skirts and beads were friendly and helpful. After thirty years at MacCurdy's they were making minimum wage plus twenty-five cents an hour. I was stupefied with boredom. I hid mystery novels under the pattern books and read in snatches. I helped grannies figure how many ounces of blue and how many of white were needed to make the sweater called Nana's Pet for their fourteen- or twenty- or twenty-seven-pound grandsons. I was calm and supportive while brides-elect dithered over a choice of lace and were snippy to their mothers. I dressed the mannequins in the store window with swaths of gorgeous fabric and many, many pins. When

MacCurdy discovered my talent for draping, he permitted me two hours a week to change the display and gave me a raise of a nickel an hour. He did the books himself every Friday morning because he didn't trust accountants. At Friday noon he signed our paycheques while his wife slapped her gloves on her purse, waiting for him to finish up and take her to lunch. She bought her clothes in Montreal, the twin sets whispered. Flew there four times a year for just that purpose. She didn't sew. When she needed buttons replaced, or hems altered, she had one of her husband's staff do it in the back room.

One August afternoon I glanced past two ladies I was helping match thread and saw a girl put two balls of yarn in her pocket and move casually towards the exit. I knew her; she'd been in a life-drawing class I'd taken. She worked part-time at the cafeteria where we drank coffee and smoked between classes. People said she saved the long butts out of the ashtrays when she cleaned up, and smoked them on her breaks. I tracked her between the rows of our autumn selection, located the manager, and then found I had nothing to say. There was a moral stance I was supposed to take, but I couldn't quite manage it. My sympathies were with the kids on the Russian trawlers, the grannies who counted change to see how much of the overpriced ribbon they could afford to buy for grandbaby's christening gown. I watched the girl slide out the front door and, at closing time, I gave my notice.

I went to work in a bar downtown. There they were again, the Russians. They put their suitcases full of polyester knit on the floor by their feet, nursed a few draft and then left in a pack. Jack, the bartender, said they had to be back on their ship by midnight. The ones who sat with a Coke all evening were some kind of watchers, KGB probably. They were responsible if any of the crew defected.

"Send 'em to Siberia if any little lambs go missing."

The waiters disliked the Russians because they seldom tipped but the customers liked them well enough. They practised words together, "beer," "cigarette," "hat." The Russians wanted big money; the Canadians wanted a deal. After a certain amount of beer everybody got flexible. Thirty dollars was the going rate but I've seen guys pay seventy or more close to curfew. There was a certain cachet in owning one of those hats and everybody lied about how little they'd paid. I wanted one but I didn't have time to bargain. Too busy wiping tables, serving beer, making change, fending off grabbers. You had to bargain; you had to invest time as well as money.

A group would come for several nights, then disappear. A week would pass, another ship would dock, another crew wanting polyester, beer and a chance to stretch their legs. One of the younger men— Yuri was his name—had a hat I particularly coveted, chocolate brown with russet highlights. He sold it early his first night, then drank and shot pool. He played for money, which was forbidden but the manager turned a blind eye as long as the players were discreet and the bets were small. Nobody would play a hustler; there was an unspoken agreement among the regulars, and newcomers followed the rules or were ostracized. Yuri won; his breaks were brilliant explosions that sent at least one ball flying into a corner pocket and from there he was almost unstoppable. He turned his winnings immediately back into beer which he shared out with everyone—so no one minded losing to him.

"That damn Yuri," they'd say, "beat the pants off me again." Pound him on the back, drink his beer and laugh. He even tipped the waiters. When the guy who bought the hat offered it to me for a "date" and I told him where to put it, Yuri tried to buy the hat back for me. The guy just laughed at him. Yuri made dismissing motions, patted me on the back, said "hat," smiled and pointed to himself. I began to think I might get one after all.

The second night he paid for two draft and had me deliver them to the KGBers, winking and shushing with his finger across my lips to let me know I wasn't to tell on him. Then he and his buddies watched like school kids who've put a frog in teacher's desk as their colleagues tried to explain to me that they most certainly hadn't ordered beer and would not pay for it. When I finally managed to convince them the beer was free—no charge, nyet, nyet, backing away with my hands open, shaking mys head and smiling—their expressions turned from indignation to consternation. The younger of the two finally pushed the beer to the far end of the table, as though he feared contamination. His companion suffered through his Coke the rest of the evening, staring sadly at the two abandoned drinks—which no one else would touch—as they went flat and tepid. When the curfew came around and everyone was being herded up the stairs, he darted back and drained one flat beer without stopping for breath. The tavern cheered.

The third evening Yuri learned the word "beautiful."

"Beautiful Anna." He took my hand and kissed it. "Hat. Beautiful hat, beautiful Anna." His friends teased him, nudged and needled him, but he ignored them, patted my shoulder, smiled and said "Hat."

When I had a moment, I watched him shoot pool. His hands were marked with white scars, small raised dashes and commas on his fingers—fish hooks, I guessed, or filleting knives; my mother's cousins were fishermen. He shoved the sleeves of his black wool sweater up to his elbows before each shot, and under the sweater his forearms were pale and muscled, as finely cut as Michelangelo's David in my History of Art text. I wondered if it would be foolish to give him some money—as a down payment. I did want one of those lovely hats, and maybe he would come through for me. He seemed to like me; perhaps I reminded him of someone he cared for—a wife or sweetheart, somebody back home reading his Cyrillic love letters in a crowded flat, waiting for his ship to dock once or twice a year. I didn't think he would just pocket the money and keep it; money seemed to be merely pieces of paper to him. Something to be got, turned into pleasure and shared. The next night I came to work prepared to put the hat transaction on a solid financial footing. Yuri didn't show. His boat had sailed in the night and no one knew when or if it might be back.

Six months later I was back in school, working weekends at the bar, when Jack called and said I'd be sorry if I didn't come down right now. It was late on a school night, I had sketches to finish, but Jack was so insistent that I went. It wasn't Yuri. It was a stranger, a polyester speculator. He gave me a hat, glossy black with silver tips, a spectacular hat.

"Yuri," he said, followed by a string of syllables I didn't understand. It was curfew time and they were leaving, four of them. I walked up the steps, followed them down Salter Street and along Barrington. I realized I hadn't paid for the hat.

"Wait."

He stopped, turned, waited for me to catch up. I held out some bills. He hesitated, then folded them and pushed them into my pocket. He took my hands, turned them slowly over and pushed his thumbs against my wrists, stroked up and down along the veins. I wasn't frightened; I was paying careful attention. I'd worked in the bar long enough to recognize lechery and this wasn't it. His clothes smelled of diesel and fish; his hair was salt and pepper scrubbing up against a knitted toque. On either side of his mouth, flesh buckled into deep folds. He was speaking, slowly and quietly, a dark river of sounds and thumbprints. I began to see how you could make love in Russian, the blocky words falling down, heavy and rich, all the edges covered in velvet. I wanted to kiss his hands, but I lacked courage. It couldn't be the right gesture.

"Thank you," I said, inadequately. "Thank Yuri, too."

"Yuri," he said quietly. He placed my hands carefully together, turned and walked down the hill and out of sight.

On the bus home I watched the slushy pavement blur under orange street lamps, leaned my forehead against the cool glass and listened carefully to the conversations of the passengers around me. I stroked the silver-tipped fur, pushed my wrists deeper and deeper into its heart.

# *Righteous Living*

Charles and Willie had been married for thirty-seven years when he retired. Willie's friends warned her that he'd be underfoot, he'd follow her around and drive her crazy. Janice Wilmont, next door, hadn't stopped complaining about her husband in the five years since he'd hung up his briefcase.

"I can't go to the bathroom without him following me out of the room to see where I'm going. If I want to have a coffee downtown with the girls I have to sneak out. Soon as he sees me put my sweater on it's 'Where are you going?' and 'How long will you be?' and then it's 'I'd better drive you.' When I'm shopping he walks up the backs of my heels, grumbling about the price of everything. The man doesn't have a life of his own. His friends are dead, senile or moved to Florida and he won't make new ones. He hangs on me like a child. It's pathetic. You'll see."

Fortunately Janice was wrong. Charles and Willie had always managed to stay nicely out of each other's way so she was relieved but not too surprised when he showed no signs of wanting to shadow her.

He developed an interest in gardening. He'd always mowed the lawn and trimmed the hedges but the gardens had been her territory, almost an extension of the kitchen. He began by doing a little weeding and within a few years had completely taken over the vegetable and herb gardens. Willie, whose arthritis had progressed to a daily nag, was pleased. She devoted her time outdoors to her flower beds. His vegetables were bigger than hers had been, more succulent—the result, he said, of strict attendance to his compost pile. It had changed from an untidy spot where she dumped her vegetable peelings to an imposing, three-chambered structure, carefully built, turned, dampened and nurtured by Charles, who allowed no one near it.

One Thursday, while Willie was at her weekly low-impact aerobics class at the Y, Charles slipped on a wet patio stone, sprained his ankle and knocked himself unconscious. Willie found him angled between a brick planter of petunias and the redwood patio chair he'd pulled down with him. The blood was the worst of it; the sight made her useless for the first few seconds. Once she'd made sure that he was breathing and had a pulse, she left him for just as long as it took to grab the cell phone from the kitchen counter and call 911. She reminded herself that head wounds bleed profusely, no matter how shallow. She knew she shouldn't move him, in case his back or neck was injured, but she balled up her sweater and pressed it against his scalp to try to stop the bleeding.

"Everything's all right," she told him. She'd read that unconscious people could sometimes hear things—noises and conversations going on around them. "You've had a bit of a fall, but I've called for help and you'll be fine. We really should replace these stones—a bit of dew or some water from the sprinkler and they're slick as ice.

"I know, I know," she continued, imagining what his unconscious mind was saying in protest. "You like the look of them, and you put a lot of work into laying them. And you think it's all the fault of cheap slippers with no tread, and the stones will weather up—but they haven't in three years, have they? And look at you. Just look at you. . . ." She faltered, wiped a hand across her eyes, then realized she'd smeared blood across her face.

The ambulance arrived, noise and lights.

"Out here," she called. "Out back."

The attendants grilled Willie about Charles' medical history as they tested and monitored him, put him in a neck brace, loaded him onto a stretcher and into the ambulance. They helped her up into the back, so she could hold his hand on the way to the Emergency. I should have changed, she thought, and washed my face, but there wasn't time. I'm enough to frighten small children. Once Charles was seen to, she'd have to find a washroom and try to clean herself up. Halfway to the hospital Charles regained consciousness and ordered them to take him home again. The attendants refused but did give in to his demand that they "turn off that damn siren!" While he was being examined, Willie stood out in the waiting room staring through the window in the direction of the parking lot. They were renovating the west wing and all the cars were herded into one corner by lines of sawhorses and red cones. A crane was smashing out one wall and the rubble tumbled down a large chute to a dump truck below. Willie saw Charles paralyzed, bedridden, mindless, coffined, buried. She saw dead gardens and tidy, hollow rooms. Trucks rumbled past, sending up clouds of dust from the crumbled masonry.

Later, some time after supper, her son arrived from Winnipeg, and, after speaking with the doctors, he took Willie home, made her tea and put her to bed. When he went back to the hospital, she got up, turned on the light and pulled Charles' bathrobe off the door hook and in under the covers with her. Terrified wails ripped up from her gut and tore at her vocal cords. She calmed herself and dried her face on his terrycloth lapel. She was shocked by the intensity of her feelings. Her affection for her husband—a pleasant, sensible fondness—had somehow insinuated itself into her bones. Like the fixative used by paleontologists to preserve dinosaur bones, it had soaked into every pore.

She went with Young Charles at eleven the next morning, taking flowers and magazines and smiles. They were going to keep Charles in the hospital for a few days; he had sustained quite a knock and his blood pressure was up. He was indignant but, lacking skill with crutches, was helpless to escape.

"If they're so worried about my blood pressure they should let me out," he said. "How can anybody relax here? The bed's too narrow, and there's nothing good to eat."

"This looks good," said Willie, picking at the salad on his lunch tray.

"That reminds me, the tomatoes need to be suckered again." He tasted a wedge of tomato and made a face. "No more flavour than the cardboard box it came in."

"I'll sucker your tomatoes this afternoon," said Willie. "It'll give me something to do now that I don't have you to clean up after."

"You miss me, do you?" he said, winking over her head at Young Charles.

The next morning Willie decided to turn his compost pile for him. She tied her sunbonnet firmly under her chin, pulled on a pair of leather-palmed work gloves and went out to the pile. Two forkfuls in, she hit the bottle. Vodka, half full. Slowly, she wiped it with her apron and stood scanning the label while her mind skipped around the yard, roping tomatoes, zinnias, sage, linden tree, rose bushes into a net of familiar things.

Willie's father had been a drinker, although she was an adult before she'd known for sure. He'd travelled as a salesman and had managed to confine his binges to the road. Eventually stories had drifted her way; in a small town, secrets seep from one conversation to another. The family seemed to think it had been kept from her mother. When Willie expressed her doubts her brothers scoffed and said Mama had never been clever enough to guess; Da had been too sly. His explanations were plausible. The bottles in his trunk were plucked from a parking lot: no civic-minded person would have left them lying there where they might break, slash tires, or injure bicycle-wheeling children. Money was often tight—but there were the repairs, breakdowns that always happened out of town, paid for in cash, no receipts because he'd worked a deal with the mechanic.

"The guy was some kind of relation to Dan MacLean. I took some stuff to Truro for him and he gave me a good deal."

"But Lauchie—a hundred dollars!"

"Could have been a lot worse, Meg. He only charged for the parts. A salesman's got to have a car, you know that."

Surely she must have suspected, thought Willie. But Meg had been admired in her small circle of friends for having "cleaned up" Willie's father before she'd married him. Maybe as long as she hadn't been faced with direct evidence of his backsliding she'd been able to maintain the illusion that she'd succeeded in reforming him.

Meg slotted alcoholics into three groups. There were the shabby old men who lurched down back streets, mumbling to themselves, spitting on sidewalks and peeing in the alleys. Then there was a collection of abandoned great-uncles and second-cousins-once-removed steadily drinking their way to oblivion in boarding houses backed up to the railroad tracks in other towns. Never seen in church, never invited to Sunday dinner at Willie's house, they were the broken twigs of the family tree. Doomed, without a wife or mother to drive them back onto the path of sobriety and righteous living. The third group consisted of alcoholics-in-waiting, the fathers (and sometimes mothers) of friends, cousins and neighbours known to take an occasional drink. They were not yet lost, but were balancing on desperately slippery slopes. The possibility of disaster lurked in every bottle, and any morning could be the one to find them washed up in a boarding house in another town.

Willie carried the bottle to the kitchen, buried it in the towel drawer and washed her hands. Then she made quiche and salad for lunch.

"I don't believe I'll go today, dear," she told Young Charles as he was getting ready to drive to the hospital.

"Don't you feel well?"

"I'm fine. I just don't think I'll go today."

"You need a rest. It's hot at the hospital and you're worn out. I'll bring you some ice cream for supper. Butterscotch ripple, right?" He kissed her and left. She went upstairs and cleaned the hall closet. She arranged the winter coats from longest to shortest. She unpacked boxes of hats, mittens, gloves and scarves, and put most of them in bags for the Salvation Army. She sat on her heels, looking up into the closet, then stood up and removed four of the newly organized coats, ones they hardly ever wore, and put them in bags too.

One evening after supper, Lauchie came home shepherding an old man from a downtown street corner. The man swayed and stumbled and Meg immediately chased the children out of the kitchen, the little ones up to bed. One by one, the older boys, and then Willie, drifted back to sit in corners or under the stairs to watch. She was thirteen; this was her first opportunity to examine a drunk in detail.

He wore a soiled, greenish jacket with mismatched buttons. They had been sewn on with white thread and the stitching had begun to pull loose. His pants were flannel, thin, limp and gaping high above his ankles; his shins pushed against the fabric like weathered rails. He sat with his feet out, braced flat against the floor in broken shoes. His hands, resting on his knees, were freckled and furred with the same thin, sandy hair that rimmed his skull. He was grey with neglect, and poverty, and the cold charity of a northern coal town.

They'd made him toast with jam and strong tea, and as the man ate, dropping crumbs and spilling tea down his front, Lauchie sat facing him, knees almost touching, with Meg's Bible open in his hand, and earnestly read out promises of salvation and strictures against the fruit of the vine.

It seemed to Willie that the man, in some way, controlled the scene. His performance was polished and automatic.

"I will love the Lord Jesus with all my heart, yes I will." He rolled his head back, his eyes travelling to some other dimension. "Yes, I am a miserable sinner; I will beg his forgiveness and love him. Yes, with all my heart, I will love my Saviour."

Lauchie looked disturbed and helpless. Finally he put the Bible away and helped the man to the door.

"He wanted money," he explained to Meg. "I knew he'd buy liquor. I thought a meal . . . I wonder if it did any good. . . ."

Meg hitched the corner of her mouth a notch tighter and got out the bottle of lysol. As she wiped the chair where the man had been sitting, Lauchie poured scalding water over and over the cup, spoon and plate the man had used. Meg watched closely to make sure he did a thorough job.

The following day Willie reorganized the basement shelves.

"Are you sure you won't come? He worries that you're ill," said Young Charles.

"I'm fine," she answered, shelving *National Geographic*s by year and month.

"Leave this, and I'll help you with it later," he suggested. "He's bored silly, and missing you. He says the nurses all whisper and he can't hear what they're saying."

"Charles," she said, "did you know—" She wasn't sure how to say it.

"Know what?"

"Your father. He drinks."

Charles laughed, then stopped, contrite. "I'm sorry. It's just— you make it sound like he's a raving alcoholic. I don't suppose he has more than one or two a week."

"Not in front of me."

"He knows you don't like it. He wouldn't want to upset you."

"Your grandfather drank."

"It's not the same. Mother, he didn't fall because he was drinking."

"I know that. What a thing to suggest about your father!" She began sorting through another pile of magazines, *Popular Mechanics*. "Tell him I turned his compost pile for him," she said. She didn't go to the hospital that evening either, and Charles didn't ask for her.

The fifth day, Young Charles brought his father home, had a quiet dinner with his parents, and then took a taxi to the airport. He had a life of his own, after all.

Charles and Willie sat in the living room, he in his easy chair, foot propped up on the ottoman, she in the rocker beside the floor lamp—in case she felt like knitting. The evening news was on the television. Charles listened for a while and then began to speak, drowning out the announcer.

"I'm an old man," he said. "I've worked hard all my life. I'm not a drunk and I don't spend a lot of money on liquor. But I enjoy a drink of an evening and I'd like to have it in my own living room like a civilized person."

The news announcer was replaced by the weatherman, who explained a map of curving lines and significant numbers. When he finished and the sportscaster began his spiel, Willie spoke.

"I'm an old woman," she said. "My arthritis gets worse every day. It's hard to get up so early in the morning and get your tea. I'd like to be able to lie in bed a bit and get up when I'm ready. I think you might get your own tea since you will get up with the birds."

A small silence. Charles offered, "I could bring you your tea in bed. To help warm your pretty bones."

"When your ankle's better," said Willie, shaking out her knitting. Charles turned his attention back to the news. Willie concentrated on the cable design she was working into the front of his new cardigan and began counting stitches under her breath.

# *Marigold*

Mary woke to the sound of slams—the light metallic snick of the aluminum kitchen door, the hearty thump as Carol forced the trunk lid down on boxes and suitcases piled too high. Mary crawled out of her sleeping bag and across the floor to the window. She looked down over the ledge and into the backyard. It was barely light; the sun was a red half-eye floating beyond the ginkgo tree. The passenger doors of the Jetta stood open but there was no sign of Carol. She must have gone indoors for another load. Mary slithered back across the floor and shimmied into her sleeping bag. Warmth still pooled at the bottom and she dipped her chilly toes into it. The floor beneath was a linoleum slab. Like sleeping in a morgue, thought Mary, like sleeping in a dungeon. She curled up, bringing the bag with her, making a quilted comma on the floor.

Carol's footsteps click-clacked across the empty kitchen. All the furniture had gone away in a small van the previous afternoon, "Albert's Moving and Storage, No Load Too Small, No Distance Too Far." Albert and his buddy, Martin, had emptied the rooms in less than two hours. Now Carol was stuffing miscellaneous boxes and bags into the car.

"I know you're awake, Mary," she yelled from the hall. "Get washed and dressed. I want to pack your sleeping bag."

It was harder getting herself up the second time. Now she knew how cold the room was, and that the sun, just scraping over the window ledge, was a fraud. Bunches of daisies and blue coneflowers on the wallpaper shivered and knotted their stems. Their leaves pulled closer together and their petals drooped. It looked like summer but it felt like fall.

"Hurry now." Carol was shaking the end of the sleeping bag, trying to roll her out. "This is the start of our big adventure. This is the first day of the rest of our lives."

"This is stupid," muttered Mary. She kicked free of the bag and sat up on the cold floor, clutching her magic talisman bag in one hand and holding her pyjama top shut with the other. "Why do *we* have to leave? We shouldn't have to leave. Make *him* leave."

"Please don't be difficult." Carol was pleading, folding and smoothing. "You know this is how it has to be. I need your help, Mary, I don't need an argument. This was your idea too, you know. Please."

Mary scrambled up, ran to the bathroom and slammed the door. Her clothes lay on the edge of the bathtub. A face cloth and towel were folded beside them. On the vanity her toothbrush, hairbrush and toothpaste were laid out in an open toiletry case. A sliver of soap they would leave behind was wet and gelid in the sink. Everything else was gone, even the curtains. It was a gamble, taking the curtains down; if he came back early and drove by the house he'd see the blank windows and know something was up.

Carol's heels went click-click past the door. High heels, stupid shoes for a getaway, thought Mary. She peeled a strip of varnish from the back of the closet door, a long skinny strip like a snake's cast-off skin. Where the varnish was gone the wood was dull and gave off a musty odour. She brushed and flossed her teeth, flicking small white spots onto the mirror, then washed her face and put on her clothes. Her pyjamas were in tatters, no buttons on the top and a big tear in the bum. She was to leave them behind too, like the soap. Carefully she folded them flat, then rolled them into two tight sausages and put them on the top shelf of the linen closet. She pushed them back as far as she could reach. Maybe the new tenants would be careless and stuff their towels up on the high shelf without looking. Her pyjamas would live quietly, hidden in the dark. Someday she would come back and look for them. When she opened the door to the hall Carol swooped in to snatch up cloth, towel, the toiletry case and its contents. Mary followed her downstairs, hand trailing the banister, over and under, feeling for gum. None. It had been cleaned again.

"Hurry." Carol's voice was tight and urgent; she clickety-ticked in and out of the downstairs rooms for one last check. Outside, the car was running.

"Where's my breakfast?" Mary wasn't ready to go yet.

"We'll get some on the road."

"He's not coming back until Sunday. That's three days. That's lots of time for breakfast."

Carol faced her daughter. "I can't eat," she said. "Not here. We have to go right now." She jerked Mary by the shoulder and pushed her towards the door. "There's food in the car if you can't wait." Carol's fingers on Mary's shoulder were glass bones. It would take nothing to snap them. Mary got in the front on the passenger's side and buckled her seat belt. When they pulled out of the yard she concentrated on peeling the paper from a cranberry–sunflower seed muffin and did not look at her disappearing street.

Once they reached the highway Carol began to babble. She speculated about the weather, the road conditions, where they might stop for breakfast. "At least an hour out of town; two would be better. I need a hundred miles between me and this town before I can eat a bite. We'll find someplace nice to stop, don't you worry. Do you want another muffin? A banana? My stomach's just a solid lump!" On and on.


At first it had been Mary who'd wanted to run away. "Why don't we just hide from the bad man?" She was six and the sight of her mother in tears had become a regular and worrisome occurrence.

"He's not a bad man. He's your daddy; he doesn't mean to hurt. He just gets angry. Running away doesn't fix anything."

"*My* daddy's dead. He's under the shiny black rock."

"Sam is your daddy now. We just need to learn to live together like a family."

Finally Carol admitted defeat and one day there was a long bus ride with suitcases and Mary's two best Barbies—one in a fur coat, the other in a leather jacket and jeans, both wearing red plastic high heels. When they got off the bus Sam was there, blocking their path with flowers for Carol and a stuffed bear for Mary. They drove back in his car, Carol crying a little, Sam talking and Mary eating chocolates in the back seat until she was sick. Presents and bruises—they swung back and forth between those two poles of his attention. One red Barbie shoe was lost and never recovered.

Sam and Carol divorced when Mary was eight, but it made little difference; he never stayed away for long. Mary began to save her allowance and kept it in her mermaid knapsack in her closet, with extra socks and underwear, ready to go. Carol found it and sat on her heels in the closet wiping her eyes and blowing her nose with bits of Mary's dirty laundry.

"We'll run away together," she promised. "Just don't you go without me. I'll save and we'll do it properly. We have to have somewhere nice to run to. I got us into this and I can get us out."

Carol was nicer to Sam then; she never argued with him, never ever let on. Mary was impressed by how sneaky her mother could be. She tried to be nicer too, to fool him, although she refused to go anywhere with him unless Carol came along. She saved the money he gave her—running money, she called it—dropping it into the glass milk bottle her Aunt Edie had given her to use as a bank. After his visits she played with the coins, stacked the loonies and quarters, nickels and dimes in towers, then knocked them down. When she finished clinking them back into the bottle, Carol put it on the high shelf in the kitchen cupboard. The sleeves of her silk kimono fell like green waterfalls past her elbows. One or the other upper arm was purpled with fingerprints. There was always a mark somewhere on Carol, on her arm, shoulder, buttock, thigh. As one faded he imprinted her anew: a helping hand gripping her a little too tightly, an accidental elbow to her ribs, a clumsy gesture that nicked her shins. Always trying to carve his initials. Always trying to make a permanent mark.

"He never hits me." She was annoyed by her sister's rants. "What bloody good would a peace bond do? What would I say to the judge? Your Honour, he's a mean little prick? I think he does it on purpose? It's easy for you to go on, Edie. He never even raises his voice, for Christ's sake!"

Mary liked Aunt Edie. She seemed likely to do something, maybe get a policeman to put Sam in jail.

"Honey, are you sure he hasn't. . . ?"

"No." Mary shook her head stubbornly. She knew what they meant. No. It was more like the way he tormented Carol. Different—and the same. A mean yank of her braid, a nippy little pinch to make her mind her manners, no skin broken, just pain and a bruise. Tickling fingers that grew bony and cruel.

"Stop! It hurts!"

"Who's a whiny little crybaby now?" He jeered at her and gave one last little jab that made a sore place in her belly.

"He's a teacher. A so-called respected member of the community," said Carol.

"He's a sadistic bully," said Aunt Edie.

Sadistic bully. Mary liked the words; she wrote them on her palm in turquoise ink.

"He's never forgiven me for divorcing him," said Carol. "He's still mad."


It was almost noon before Carol would stop for breakfast. Mary ate eggs, pancakes and bacon while Carol nibbled at some toast, drank coffee and smoked. Her avalanche of words had slowed to a trickle. Her eyes were too heavy; the skin around them was bruised with fatigue.

"I wish you were sixteen, baby," she said. "I could use another driver to spell me. I don't think I slept a wink last night."

"Me neither," said Mary, sympathetically, although it wasn't true. "We've come a long way." It was her turn to be bright and cheerful. She wasn't mad anymore. After all, it had been her idea to run away. It was just that it had been scary when Albert and Martin took all their furniture. She hadn't thought they'd run away with furniture; they might *never* come back. "Let's take the scenic route." She pointed to her place mat, a plasticized map with the coastal route marked in red and decorated with silhouettes of herons, leaping fish and sea lavender.

"Sure, baby." Carol lit another cigarette, blew out the smoke and smiled. "We'll be on the road a week anyway. We might never get a chance to see the country like this again so we should make the most of it."

It was beginning, slowly, to feel like an adventure. A trip she could write about in her new school. "My Trip Across Canada," or something like that. An ordinary sort of family adventure that anyone might have. All the marks would fade and they would look like regular people. On their skin and in their eyes.

Mary held Carol's hand on the way across the parking lot, swinging high and swinging low. The handle of the door was hot in the sunshine and the car smelled like bananas and old cigarettes.

"Whew. We'd better crack the windows and let in a little fresh air." Carol fanned the interior with a map. Mary settled in her seat, squirming until her clothes settled properly, then leaned over and turned on the radio. Carol pulled out into the traffic and took the first left to the Seaside Trail. Mary spun the dial through the blips and squawks until she found some music she liked. Ten miles down the Trail they came hard up against a funeral procession. A dozen polished cars moved a sedate fifteen kilometres an hour behind a hearse.

"Damn," said Carol.

"Why damn? Is it bad luck to be behind a funeral?"

"Of course not. But they'll crawl along for miles and we'll be stuck behind them."

"We could pass them."

"It's disrespectful to pass a funeral. They can't be going too far. There must be a graveyard somewhere near, otherwise they'd be on the main highway. We'll just be patient. Open your window all the way so we'll get a cross-breeze."

Mary wound down her window. Two girls on the back seat of

the car in front of them turned to stare at her. Both wore their hair in braids, tied with blue ribbons. One lifted a lace-gloved hand and waved, until the other grabbed her and made her stop.

When Mary was seven, her grandmother, her real father's mother, died. She and Carol went to the grandparents' house early, wearing their Sunday clothes. Mary's hair was combed back straight and shiny, pinned behind her ears with white barrettes. She wore new sandals. Sam came, too, although he was no relation to anybody.

Mary heard the whispers.

"What's that joker doing here?"

"Shush. He's here for Mary."

"Mary don't need him. He's not her real father. We're her family. Nobody needs him."

"Hush, for God's sake. Make a scene at your own mother's funeral, why don't you! Shame us all, that'd be nothing new."

The grown-ups, in black suits and crepe dresses, were gathered in the kitchen. The crying was finished for the moment; they were pouring a little something from a bottle into their tea. Carol was enveloped in a circle of in-laws. Sam went out on the back steps for a smoke. Mary's cousin, Bryan, took her to see the body.

The coffin was set on a stand in the front parlour; the top half was folded back. The grandmother was dressed in royal blue lace. Her eyes were closed, hands folded, mouth lipsticked shut. Her skin, sallow in life, had been tinted a rose-petal pink. Mary thought she looked pretty healthy. But dead.

"Touch her," said Bryan. "She's cold."

Was this allowed? She could get into trouble. "No," said Mary. Bryan went off to the kitchen to scrounge for cake. After he'd gone, Mary dirty-double-dared herself, then touched a hand. It felt like uncooked pork roast, chilled from the fridge.

The minister arrived, the cups were hastily rinsed and stacked in the sink, and everyone assembled for the service. The crying began again, but softer now. The family was musical and there was a bit of competition in the harmonizing of the hymns. Everyone tried to drown out Cousin Anna who was tone-deaf and would spoil the effect if allowed.

The grey-gloved undertaker closed the coffin and arranged the pallbearers, the husky young cousins and grandsons who did the lifting, and the frail elders who leaned into the polished wood for support when they stumbled. Mary and the rest of her relatives followed in dignified order. The coffin was loaded into the hearse, the relatives divided into cars, and they started off. The procession was quietly thrilling; it *was* a kind of a parade. They drove past staring grubby children who finger-counted the cars to gauge the importance of the deceased. Mary wanted to wave, like the Queen Mother, but knew exactly what kind of trouble she would get into and restrained herself. She held a tragic profile up to the window until her neck began to ache and then quit to eat contraband Smarties with Bryan and his little sister, Shelley.

It was cold at the cemetery. The sun appeared and disappeared as flimsy clouds moved to the east. Sam held Mary's shoulder in his public grip, to keep her from fidgeting. The coffin was lowered into the dark hole; the shovelful of dirt struck the lid with a sound of little pebbles. Mary imagined her grandmother flinching, then remembered that she could not. She was in heaven with God, looking down. So they said. Bad enough Him spying on me, thought Mary, now she's at it too. They stopped for a moment at her real father's grave so Mary could put a rose on it. Mary wasn't sure where he was. Not spying on her, of that she was certain.

The funeral procession turned off and all the shiny cars dipped under a painted wooden arch that said "Glenholme Cemetery. Salvation Belongeth Unto The Lord." Carol sped a little to make up for lost time.

Twenty minutes later they ran into some light rain and the road began to feel greasy beneath the swishing tires. As soon as she could, Carol took them back to the highway. When they stopped for gas Mary got in the back seat and tried to nap. Tricky, with a seat belt that must be kept on at all times. She arranged herself this way and that among the boxes and bags, with a pillow under her cheek. She dozed, read a bit, dozed again.

Carol was singing an old Stones' tune, and tapping the wheel with the flats of her fingers to keep the rhythm.

Mary saw, out the side window, Sam's face—startled, shocked, then snatched away. Carol continued singing, softly, so she wouldn't wake Mary. She hadn't seen him; she hadn't noticed his car heading in the other direction, passing in a small convoy. Mary stared out the back window, saw red brake lights flashing as the cars were forced to slow down to let him out of line. A toy car in the distance, a little tinker of a thing, he U-ed on the highway and came speeding back. He'd seen the plastic roof rack, the boxes high in the back seat, and known instantly what they were doing. Now he's really mad, thought Mary; now he's coming to kill us. Carol was speeding a little, steel-belted radials eating up the miles, swallowing the white lines to freedom; she sang and tapped. Sam was gaining. Mary could see his foot: one hundred percent cotton knit sock, tan loafer pressing down hard on the gas pedal.

Mary pulled her talisman bag from her back pocket. She'd made it herself, from instructions in a library book. She'd cut up her favourite T-shirt and used part of the back where the fabric was unstained and silky smooth. Five lucky pieces, centred, folded and wrapped, then tied with a ribbon from Carol's lingerie drawer. A small white stone from the beach where her real father had learned to swim when he was seven; a brass button with a green glass centre she'd found in a bin at Frenchies; a barred feather the man at the museum said was from a horned owl; a five-yen piece with a hole in it that her great-uncle Melvin told her was lucky; a small glass vial with a plastic stopper, a reddish brown stain on the bottom. It had contained a contact lens: her best friend, Ayesha, had a sister who wore disposables and they'd scavenged two vials from the garbage. They'd stuck their fingers with a pin and squeezed and squeezed to get enough blood so they could mix it and each have a little. Mary rubbed the bag. "Please don't let him catch us, amen."

They were on an older stretch of highway now; there were bumps and curves, but nothing seemed to slow him. The road got worse by the second—the shoulders thinning to dirt, the houses crowding closer to the edge. Late-summer gardens were brilliant with colour and the tomato plants gave off red sparks of fruit as they passed. Carol had begun to slow on the curves but Sam was taking them much too fast, jerking back from the shoulder each time his wheels threatened to spin off the edge. He was too good a driver; in a few seconds it would be over. Mary reached out through the back window and pulled the highway straight. The curve Sam was following ceased to exist and his car sailed off into a field, swirled up a cloud of startled crows who'd been picking at the corpse of a rabbit, and crashed into a low stone wall. Sam kept travelling, out through the windshield in a crystal flash, and came to rest in the flower garden on the other side of the wall. Mary let go of the road and it snapped back into shape.

Carol had changed tunes, getting a little carried away, forgetting that she was trying to let Mary sleep. All the sounds had been gathered in and buried in Mary's ears. All the breaking, smashing, screaming cries of glass and metal. Sam lay face down, his head under a mass of deep pink roses, his legs broken and shoeless. One arm stretched out to a yellow and orange border. Crackerjack marigolds shook their petals like confetti into his open palm.

The wind funnelling in through the air vents had ruffled and feathered Carol's fair hair. Her long neck was much too thin for her seedpod head. How easily it could snap, thought Mary, or a set of stairs ripple out from under as she climbed with a load of groceries, or a curb tumble her into oncoming traffic as she waited for the light to change. Mary had a second five-yen piece and she decided to put it in a talisman bag for her mother as soon as possible. With a stone from a beach on the Pacific Ocean and dried marigold petals from a garden they would plant together. They would be safe. Everything would be fine. She gazed at her mother's pale nape and the earnest hunch of her shoulders; a tender ache bloomed in her throat and would not be swallowed.

# Homarus Americanus

Becca steps off the bus, stands back from the huffing diesel fumes and hangs over her toes to unkink her spine. The driver is tossing bags and bundles to the ground; she pulls hers out from the pile and walks through the back door of the depot to find Annie. They stop for a flat of beer and cigarettes on the way home.

"For Ned," says Annie. She pulls off the main road to a twenty-kilometre gravelled curve and slide that fetches up a two-storey, white, piazzaed house.

"I didn't realize the house was this big." Becca has seen pictures.

"Big and drafty," says Annie.

In the three years since Annie moved down the coast Becca has seen her twice, both times in the city. Annie'd tried to explain, Becca'd tried to understand why her bright older sister dropped out of law school to go fishing.

"Come for a visit," she said. "Come and see how I live. It suits me. Odd, but there it is. Serendipity saved me from a life of power, success and financial reward."

Becca's parents think Annie needs de-programming. They've financed this trip, rather niggardly, thinks Becca-the-starving-student; she's had to pay for the wine she's brought as a gift from her own meagre funds. She is to cess out the situation. Her parents are out of patience, waiting for Annie to come back, chastened, to rejoin the real world.

Becca hauls her bag from the truck and stands, looking around. The house has a bit of a lean; the paint is flaking here and there. Tomato seedlings are drinking sunshine in flats on the piazza. A grey tabby on the rail twitches her tail back and forth, teasing the elderly Lab snoozing below. He sighs and pushes his nose deeper into his paws.

The property, on a point on the north end of a small bay, touches the sea on three sides, from the sparkling wavelets in the inner cove to the green glassy slide over the reef by the entrance to the deep blue roll that thunders all the way to Ireland.

Becca quotes her father: "The end of the civilized world as we know it." She is going to be a failure as a spy, but she's known that from the beginning. She doesn't understand Annie's choices but Annie is a hero. Annie, unlike Becca, seems to know what she wants.

The house is clean but disorderly. Fishing clothes are hung everywhere to dry. Rubber boots take up an entire corner. Plants sprawl and bloom. Becca is introduced to Ned, who came to fish for Tom a few years back and stayed.

"He's family, now," says Annie.

Ned has a room off the kitchen, and, to please Annie, he smokes outside. Becca has met Tom, in the city, the previous winter.

"You'll be coming with us in the boat." They take it for granted.

"Will it be rough? I'd like to come but not if it's rough."

"Get seasick?" Ned is sympathetic.

"I don't know. I don't want to find out."

"I used to get sick, when I was young. Puked between every trawl for years."

Becca is aghast. "Why did you go fishing, then?"

"Had no choice, my girl."

By nine everyone else is in bed asleep. Becca reads, quietly turning pages. She wishes she could sleep—her alarm is set for quarter to four—but her body is not convinced she is going to do this foolish thing and it will not shut down. When the alarm trips, she struggles up, feeling as if she's been slugged. Annie has laid out a pile of clothing for her: wool sweaters, long johns, wool socks, even a hat.

"It's cold out on the water in May. You'd be surprised."

It is cold. Cold enough to slap her wide awake as she stands on deck, hauling in the stern lines with Annie in the pre-dawn light. Five boats leave the wharf in single file, engines roaring, then split off in separate directions. Tom steers the boat to the southeast as Annie and Ned manhandle bait trays into position.

The sun bleeds a fine rose line at the horizon, underpaints the cloud bank, then flares up, a bloated peony at the edge of the eastern sea. The water below Becca's enthralled gaze is overlaid with burgundy-blue plums.

"Look, Annie! Look at the colours!"

"I tried to photograph them at first." Annie smiles at her. "I still try to paint them but I get so frustrated. It looks like I've been doing acid. Every imaginable colour is out here but you have to be a fisherman or a sailor to see what I'm trying to do. When the sun comes up on a grey morning the light spills around the boat like gold coins on a brushed aluminum plate. When I paint it, it looks ridiculous. Everybody knows what the ocean looks like—green waves with whitecaps and a little spume for effect. A blue pool with a pretty sunrise fanning across one end. Nothing like that." She points to the purple plums which become bloody entrails scrolling across a wrinkled grey sheet as the sun turns a brilliant orange.

To the port side is the point, a long, low black smudge with a green eye winking at the wharf's end. Farther down the coast, rising from the pulp mill, is a yellowish brown cloud. Its visible thickness parallels the depth of the land beneath it as it stretches away to the south. It is a vile sight, a piss stain on a water-colour morning.

Ned gives Becca a job and ongoing commentary.

"Stay away from the rope. Them coils can jump up and twist around your feet and before you know it, you're overboard. If you're lucky, you smash your head on the way down so you ain't conscious when you start to drown. The traps, see, pull you to the bottom and we'd never get you back up in time. You'd best stand over here." He hands her a bander and shows her how to pick up and hold a lobster with one hand and band it with the other.

"Them big crushers, now, they'll take a man's finger off." He holds up a crab, carapace smashed, legs dangling, raw meat oozing from its wounds, to show what a big lobster can do if not properly banded. "Lobsters is cannibals."

Tom is using fresh mackerel for bait. The smallest ones go into bait bags whole, but most need to be cut in half. Ned chops them up with a hatchet, their livers, stomachs and gonads squirting viscous fluids across the cutting board and through the air. Their skins shimmer like abalone shells: pink and green, turquoise, violet and silver. Black markings spill messages along their flanks. Why cut up chickens, thinks Becca; why read entrails, messy, hot and stinking; why not read mackerel skins? ROY, she reads; ONO, says the next. How has civilization missed this, she thinks. Mackerel are the soothsayers; mackerel are oracles from our watery origins. LOW, says one, and then the mackerel with the message for her—JOY, it proclaims. It's written on a fish, it's real, it's achievable. She paws through the bait tray, blood and guts flying; she is looking for the one that says BECCA.

Ned is chatting again.

"Lobsters ain't just green and red. Look close, you'll see all colours. All except purple. See the blue here, and the green; there's yellow and white and orange. Brown and black, too. Usually more of one or two but most have a little of all them colours. I've got one I'll show you at home, black as midnight unless you shine a bright light hard on 'er. And blue. Got two blue, a market and a canner. Beauties. Got one mostly like vanilla pudding. Pretty near all white. Man offered me a hundred for that one; I told 'im, stick a few more zeros on. You've seen the bright orange ones, like they been new painted, and then there's the regular orangey-green ones. I figure somewheres there's a yellow one. See the colour here under this here elbow? That's yellow as butter. Somewheres there's one mostly all this colour. But I never seen it, not yet anyways.

"What you don't want to do, see, is cook 'em. My Jesus, no. Put 'em in hot water and they turn red; then you ain't got your blue lobster no more, have you? What you do is you bury it in a anthill, see? A big lively anthill and then you leave 'er there awhile. Oh, I dunno, check it every now and again. The ants clean out all the meat and it don't get bleached 'cause the sun can't get at it. When it's ready you take it home and wash it three, four times and when it's dry you dip it in some urethane. Couple coats keeps it real good."

"Want to pick a few traps?" Annie calls over. "Watch your feet around the rope."

Gingerly, Becca steps up to the washboard. The traps are alive with creatures. The lobsters are put aside to be measured and banded; the rest go back to the sea. Annie cartwheels them over the side and tells Becca to do the same. Most are rock crabs, tenacious little buggers that strip the bait and fight Becca's efforts to dislodge them. There are sculpins, poisonous spines erect, bug eyes glaring, whiplashing about in an attempt to impale her. The flatfish slap across the trap floor in a frenzy or hold themselves rigid as kites in a stiff wind. They vibrate and suck air through their tiny misshapen mouths. Rock eels, she decides, are the neurotics of the sea; they thrash and silently wail, wriggle and coil themselves around her arm, squirm and slither until they've braided themselves into the trap walls. One rock eel is a panic attack, two is mass hysteria, three is a ward in nineteenth-century Bedlam. She'd like to leave them for Ned, but she doesn't want Annie to think she's a wimp.

As she waits for the next trap Becca leans over the edge, watching the crabs flail their way back to the bottom. The sun is behind her; the rays strike the back of her head and seem to radiate from her reflection in all directions. She is wearing a halo; she is a mediaeval saint. She spreads her arms beatifically over the waves.

"Bless you," she murmers to all the little souls tumbling below her.

"Heads up." Annie slings another trap along the washboard to be picked and baited.

Now the sun is a quarter-way up the sky and has burned off most of the fog. The wind stirs, riffling the water to chops and jags and angles. The sun caroms off tips and edges: diamond fields surround the boat. Annie goes forward and returns wearing sunglasses. She hands Tom a pair and gives one to Becca.

"Put these on and don't stare at the water. It'll give you a hellish headache."

"What about Ned?"

"It don't bother me none. I can't work in 'em. The spray gets all over."

"He'd rather fry his retinas." Annie shakes her head, disapproving.

His answer is to wing a crab past her left ear. Becca notices, though, that the myriad wrinkles around his eyes are drawn close and folded together like a drawstring purse, leaving only a thin slit through which he squints at the world.

The wind is still rising. The boat lifts and falls beneath her. It's getting harder to keep her balance. At Tom's command she goes back in the corner to band and measure lobster, to stay out from underfoot, away from the treacherous rope and flying traps.

Annie and Ned roll and dip from trawl to trawl, picking, baiting, hauling the traps up and shoving them off, all the while maintaining balance and speed, staying out of each other's way. Their feet constantly move around and away from the lethal, snaking coils of rope; they are a pair of dancers from a leftist People's Troupe, performing a washboard pas de deux.

But now Becca has a problem.

"I have to pee, guys."

"The head's down below, up near the bow. The green door with oil gear hanging on it. Don't crack your head when the boat rolls."

The green door? She'd thought it was a storage cupboard for life jackets. She'll never get in there with all her clothes on. She struggles out of her jacket and oil pants. The ceiling isn't more than four and a half feet from the floor—deck, she corrects herself. She lowers her jeans and backs in. The bowl is a foot off the floor; her knees are up around her ears. She closes the door, turning her feet sideways so it will shut. At least she can't lose her balance and tumble off. She is a jammed-in sardine. The marine architect responsible for this, she decides, is skinny, short, and perverse. The toilet flushes with a hand pump conveniently located to the rear and just out of reach. She opens the door, gets up, whacks her head and staggers out. By the time she's back on deck, twenty minutes have passed.

"How do you stand it?" she asks Annie.

"I drink as little as possible and try to avoid it altogether. The last boat we had didn't have a head. If you think this is bad, imagine perching on a plastic bucket in a pitching sea. The guys just drop the front of their oil pants and piss over the side. That son-of-a-bitch Freud wasn't all wrong. I suffer from penis envy every time I'm fishing and have to pee."

At eight-thirty, Tom yells "Lunch!" and shuts the engine off. Annie ties the buoy line to the stern so they're anchored by the trawl they've just shoved back into the water. Becca is ravenous. For the second time that day she eats. Two sandwiches, three squares, a banana, a scant mouthful of coffee.

"It's barely breakfast time." She's surprised at her appetite.

After lunch the wind blows steady, coming first from the south, gradually shifting to the west. Becca stays in her corner, measuring and banding, filling empty bait bags, rocking and rolling and feeling relieved and a little proud of her placid and well-behaved stomach.

"Not seasick, are you?" Ned is watching.

"Of course not," she says grandly.

"Good girl."

Maybe I'll get a tattoo, she thinks. An anchor on my thigh. Discreet but sexy. She begins to hum "Make and Break Harbour." She loses track of time. The sky clouds over and they sail in and out of ragged patches of fog being slowly blown to the east. Years are passing; she thinks she's drifted into a paranormal ocean and will spend eternity in an ill-fitting rubber suit with bits of old bait in her hair.

Then they are finished and Tom is turning the boat to sail back to land where, amazingly, the sun still shines and it's barely eleven o'clock in the morning. The trip back is fast and lively. The spray breaks against the side of the cabin and shoots a peal of water droplets along the washboard. Wisk, woosh. When Becca stands so that the sun is behind her, each spray strings a rainbow, a brief flashing prism, a three-foot-long miracle. She counts, "Fifty-nine, sixty, sixty-one. I will have fantastic luck. This is like a thousand cranes, but better. I will be offered a great summer job for big bucks. My plants will be in bloom when I get back. I will meet a wonderful man who will adore me." She knows this is nonsense but the magic of armloads, boatloads of rainbows makes her giddy. "One hundred and three, one hundred and four, one hundred and five . . ."

The process of selling the fish, buying fresh bait, cleaning and tying up the boat takes longer than Becca expects. Tom and Annie are most particular about getting every little bit of old bait washed off and out the scuppers.

"If you think it smells bad now," says Annie, "imagine what a couple of weeks of June weather does to old bait stuck in the bilge."

Becca walks the length of the wharf at a pitch and stagger. Attuned to the dip and return of the deck, her legs will not adjust to the implacable solidity of dry land; her feet slam down with spine-jarring finality or paw the air a few inches above ground.

It's past noon when they enter the house, shedding boots, damp sweaters and jackets with soggy sleeves. After a quick wash and a few mouthfuls of whatever is quickest to hand, Ned goes off to his room, Tom and Annie go upstairs to nap. Becca is too tired to eat.

"I think I'll just lie on the couch for a bit," she mumbles. There is barely time to pull an afghan to her shoulders before she spirals into a deep black hole.

When consciousness returns, with the jerk of a buoy smacking the surface of the sea, she can't remember who or where she is. Her muscles aren't taking incoming calls and her mind has the uncomplicated focus of a snail working its way through a head of lettuce. She is distracted by the sunlight on the opposite wall, bemused by the shape of the spider plant hanging at the end of the couch. Slowly she gathers herself together, begins a dialogue with her arms and legs.

Annie is in the kitchen making salad.

"Have a beer. A few friends from down the road are coming for supper. We work hard all week, and the weather's not often as good as it was today, so on Saturday we like to party a little. It's the only night of the week we can stay up late, at least until the season's over."

Tom comes in from the backyard and rummages in the fridge. He opens a beer and hands it to Annie, raises a questioning arc of brow to Becca.

"I'm fine, thanks." She hoists her bottle.

He snaps the cap off a second beer, takes a long swallow and then stands behind Annie to slowly knead the muscles over and under her shoulder blades. She closes her eyes and leans into it, hands poised above the salad bowl. After a few minutes, he drifts back outdoors to check the cooker.

Annie is busy at the salad again, ripping lettuce and humming, her face serene as sunlight on the cove at slack tide. Becca thinks of her own unsatisfactory love life and is ashamed of a flash of sour jealousy.

Three weeks ago she and her boyfriend had gone out to dinner, an artificial anniversary, an attempt to pump some life into their flagging affection for one another. They'd ordered lobster, in a harbourside restaurant: split carcasses piled with de-shelled, chopped meat drowning in a thick pool of sauce, overpriced wine, smarmy waiters and a roomful of strangers sitting too close to their table—chewing, slurping and discussing, too loudly, things Becca'd rather not have heard.

"It was all through him, dear. My sister-in-law—you know, Harry's wife—is a nurse in the O.R. She told me when they opened him up the stench was unbelievable!"

She describes the meal to Annie. It was not a success, she says.

"That's no way to eat lobster," says Annie, launching into poetry. "Listen. To eat lobster you need: a sunny yard; a picnic table or two and a lot of newspapers; good friends—say, three to a dozen; three or four lobsters and a bottle of wine (or a half-dozen beer) per person. One huge salad in chunks (so you can eat it by hand) with a simple oil-and-vinegar dressing; bread—fresh, crusty, sliced if you prefer but torn in chunks is better for sopping up the melted butter and lobster juice.

"Cook the lobster—you know how to do that. Melt a pound of butter, spread the table with newspaper. Open the papers wide and layer them thick. Put the salad in a couple of big bowls and the butter in a couple of small ones. Put them, and the bread, around the outer edges of the table. Dump the lobster in the middle. Open the beer, pour the wine. The wine should be white, any old favourite with enough backbone to stand up to the fish. If you pour it into wineglasses, sooner or later it will get knocked over; serve the wine in a good chunk of a glass.

"When you shell lobster in a restaurant they give you clever little tools and a stupid bib. You don't need that stuff. Wear an old shirt. Grab all the kitchen shears, hammers and forks you can find. If you're short on hammers, a clean rock will do.

"Lobster is a feast for *all* your senses. The tastes are obvious but there is so much more. The aroma of hot lobster dipped in butter, the exclamation of the vinagrette, the bouquet of the wine, the yeasty exhalation of the beer. Colours: incandescent orange and red, glistening greens, bowls of melted sunlight. The crunch of salad, the snick of bottle caps, the crack and smash of carapace yielding up its tender secrets. Taste the wine; don't sip, for pity's sake. Take a mouthful. Roll it around, bathe your taste buds, let your tongue wriggle and squirm in ecstasy. Feel the heat of the sun on your back, the icy flow of beer, the slow, languorous sidle of your tongue tracing a butter dribble's path from your elbow to your wrist. Eat a little too much."

Becca follows Annie's instructions, particularly the part about eating too much. The sleepy afternoon birds background the blissful sighs, moans and gentle grunts of a crowd that has abandoned language as a medium too thin and cerebral to express their pleasure.

"It's a grand life, if you don't weaken," sighs Ned.

Afterward, Annie dumps the implements into the bowls and leaves them on the counter. Tom tosses the shells onto the compost pile while Ned folds the newspapers with the mess inside and puts that on the compost pile, too. A few of the more particular guests rinse their faces, hands and arms with the garden hose. Becca goes to the house to look for a bigger pair of pants. When she comes out, the drinks are fresh and the group is ambling, lazily, down the paths of old, familiar topics: fishing, politics, music. She pours herself more wine, sits back to sip and listen. Eventually the conversation devolves to a rehash of The Meaning of Everything. With the insouciance of regulars they poke and prod the carcass, ever hopeful of finding some juicy knuckle not yet chewed.

Annie comes over to sit beside her.

"How are you, now?" she asks, brushing Becca's hair back from her forehead.

Becca smiles, ruefully. "Full. Too full, and a little bit smashed. Is your life always this idyllic?"

"Sometimes. Usually not."

"You seem to belong here. On the boat. In this house. At the end of the civilized world."

"Most of the time I feel centred. Here and now, Becca. Here and now is the only place to be."

Above and to Becca's left a hummingbird is draining a bleeding-heart bush. His chest glints; his wings veil the air around him. In the middle of the butter and lobster haze, the ruby flitting among emerald leaves, the lace of lazy voices, crisp swallow of wine, cool breeze on her skin, there is a focus—an elegantly balanced harmony, a perfection of time and space that is the essence of being. She can almost feel it, shimmering above her in the evening air.

# Leap Year

Wednesday

There was this woman on the bus sneezing and coughing, you'd think she'd stay home with a cold like that, keep her germs to herself, but no, some people have to share. I moved as far away from her as I could even though it stinks of diesel down the back every time somebody opens the rear door. Still, you can't get a cold from diesel fumes. I get flu shots every fall, they help some but they're not much against a cold. I prefer sitting up front so I can see when we're getting handy the mall and have time to get buttoned and my gloves on, so I'm not rushed getting off. Drop a glove and someone's sure to step on it, slushy boots smack down before you can get to it. Early afternoon is a good time, not too busy after the lunch crowd leaves. Nobody in the stores except for a few old dears holding price tags up to their bifocals and some mothers with little ones in aluminum strollers you can fold up and hook over your arm.

I like to drop in to Sobey's at about three and sample what's new—little chunks of Haagen-Dazs bars, sausage patties they fry up right there in the aisle. The bread's not much, they never offer samples of decent bread—it's the white fog with the ineluctable marg. Dips are not too bad, onion or garlic and different-shaped little crackers to scoop them up with. Orange juice in tiny cups, almost enough to wet your tongue. Between this and that it will hold you till supper. Today they had spicy Mexican fish sticks and a new kind of cookie—double chocolate raspberry something. I almost missed the bus home. Met Dorrie in produce and talked too long by the Ugli fruit, then caught my bag on the way out the main doors—the plastic broke and spaghetti noodles shot out and fanned over the pavement. Had to carry the toilet paper home without a bag. I don't like that, it looks tacky. Bought myself a pocket knife with two blades, a bottle opener and a tiny pair of scissors.

Friday

Sale on at Big Steel, I must have tried on a dozen tops before I had enough. There were some nice gloves at Sears but the girl kept hanging on me making suggestions, flashing that incandescent smile they put on with their name tags. Leather makes me itch, I told her, then went to Shoppers, bought some ASA and waterproof adhesive tape. Looked through all the quilting magazines on the rack. I definitely prefer appliqué to patchwork; who'd buy a bunch of fabric, then chop it up into tiny squares and triangles, then sew it all back together again anyway? Sounds like a make-work project to me.

Saturday

I don't usually go on Saturdays, the place is full of kids in nose rings and ineffable hair; they mill around in groups and you can't get past them. No harm in them but they horse around and you can't get by. The 6/49 was worth nine million bucks though and I always get my tickets from the woman in the booth by the South Street entrance, we have the same first name and we even look something like. I'm convinced she's lucky for me and when I hit it big I'm going to give her ten percent—she doesn't know this, it's going to be a HUGE surprise. I'll just stroll in cool as a cucumber in my same old everyday jeans and jacket with maybe five or six strings of those tiny little diamonds set in gold wrapped around my waist for a belt and hand her the cheque and say, "Thanks, Sally. You've been lucky for me so I'm returning the favour." Then just walk away. Just like that. Walk away. Anyway, God knows where my head was Friday, I forgot to get my tickets so I had to go back Saturday morning. She wasn't there, I mean Sally, she must have the weekend off so I probably won't win. If I do, though, I'll still give her the ten percent. I mean luck is cumulative, I think she's been building me luck for some time so if I won it'd still be her doing. I didn't hang around long after I got my ticket. Grocery shoppers wandering through the place in a daze, little ones crying to ride the rockets and plastic bulldozers for a quarter. I got a pack of #11 needles for Muma and some space blankets from Canadian Tire and got the hell out.


Monday

Had to get new skate laces—no point sitting around on your butt, spreading out on cheap carbohydrates. I go to the rink twice a week for a few hours. Nothing fancy, just around and around to "The Blue Danube" and "Good Night Irene." There was this guy at Coles signing books. People were lined up with fresh copies waiting for him to scribble his John Henry inside. I had a look at the book, thirty-five bucks for hardcover *plus* all the taxes. A bunch of people had comments printed on the back. "A coming-of-age novel of sweetness and savage clarity." Coming-of-age, that means the kid discovers sex, finds out his folks are screwing around, and then some old dear whose special pet he is kicks off. Plus there's drinking in the family and a pervert who can't keep his hands off the kids. "The gritty realism of a Maritime boyhood." I could write a book myself about the gritty realism of a few Maritime boys. My first boyfriend Derek Mailer, for example. I wanted him to take me to the junior high dances, he wanted to get his hand under my shirt. We negotiated. After three months he got a better offer from Cath MacKinnon, her that's a denturist now, in that clinic at the mall. Doesn't put her hands in my mouth, let me tell you. I see Derek around here and there but we just nod. It's a little embarrassing to be reminded how desperate I was to get to those dances. Like they were such a big deal.

### Wednesday

Louise asked me to pick up some shampoo and mouthwash. She won't go herself—to work and back, that's it. You have to get back out in the real world, I say, start living again. I go to the mall for her because she has panic attacks in the parking lot. Thinks he'll see her and follow her home. He's five hundred miles away, I tell her, he doesn't know you have relatives here, how would he guess where you ran to? By now he's found some other woman to smash when every little thing doesn't go his particular way. She's thinking of seeing a therapist at the hospital where she works. I encourage her, whatever it takes. Christ, she's twenty-six and she lives like a hermit, night light on in her cave and a chair tipped under the door handle. He broke more than her ribs, I'd say. When Bert and I got divorced it was simple: he got the car, I got the furniture. He called me a bitch, I called him worse. Nobody got hit. End of story. Waterproof matches, $2.99 for a big box sealed in plastic—you never know when you might need something like that. I put them in the junk drawer next to the extra candles and the five-in-one screwdriver.

### Friday

The first Friday of every month the Clip Joint has a sale, eight bucks for a cut, junior stylist of course but some of them are pretty good and they have to practise on somebody. Muma and Louise have a neighbour come in but I'd rather go to the mall. Bette has, shall we say, a colourful conversational style. I can listen to her go on about her bowel obstructions or I can listen to Kymberlea and Krystalle talk about where they went Saturday night, what they wore and how much they drank. The thing about a bad haircut is that it always grows out and the thing about a good haircut is you'll never get it done exactly the same way again. Melanie, one of my girl-friends, has been trying for seven years, every jeezlus hairdresser in this county and the next, to get her hair cut like this guy who moved to Montreal did for her sister's wedding. Give it up, I tell her, let it go, face reality. You'll die after wasting your whole life chasing after this inimitable haircut, then the guy who does up the corpses for the undertaker will be the guy who moved to Montreal—you'll look down from heaven (or up, whatever) and he'll have fought with his boyfriend that morning and he'll botch it and you'll be buried in a dork haircut. That's life, I tell her, that's the way life is. Anyway, this cut I got isn't bad, for eight bucks I can live with it until next time.

## Monday

Grey and I went out Saturday—there's a change. Usually he comes over with beer and pizza and we watch TV with Muma until she goes to bed. When she starts to snore we sneak up to my room. I know it's crazy but it's Muma's house after all and she wouldn't like it if she knew. Fortunately she's half deaf and sleeps like the dead. Louise doesn't care what we do. We went to a bar because this band playing there, The Young and the Jobless, is a bunch of guys Grey went to school with—well, two of them anyway. So we got in free and had a few draft. The band wasn't bad, played a lot of old stuff I knew the words to. It was one of those crowds, people sang along. They used to play at some of the high school dances—I sort of remember them but back then I was into hockey players, not musicians. Grey lives at home too, with his parents and his youngest sister. When he finishes his training course, if he gets on as a driver at this ambulance service, he's going to get his own apartment again. It's hard moving back home when you've been on your own so long but what can you do? He's got child support and he pays on time or I wouldn't have anything to do with him, bet your ass. Since they cut back on his hours he's as impecunious as the rest of us and he's one of the lucky ones; he's still got a job. Grey's name is really Greystoke, but you never heard it from me. His dad was a big Tarzan fan.

## Wednesday

Well, it's not great but it's better than a kick in the head with a frozen boot. Three nights a week at the Busy Bee Laundromat. Mop the floors, make change, do up the laundry people leave. You can do your own there too as long as the other stuff's done up and you bring your own soap and bleach. Minimum wage and no benefits, they damn well shouldn't quibble if you do your own. Louise says she'll drop ours off and pick it up in her car. I can't take it all on the bus. EI takes most of what I earn off my cheque but even so I figure it might lead to a full-time job. God, it's boring. Everybody smokes or paces except the old dears who come in pairs and put their heads together in a corner while they slander their old men in idiomatic dialogue. The TV is broke, good thing I read. I go to the library once a week and I carry the *Reader's Digest* in my back pocket—mostly for the jokes and "It Pays to Enrich Your Word Power." Stopped at the mall on the way to work, there was a sale on detergent, six bucks for the industrial-size Sunlight, however many kgs that is. I never know what kgs mean. About ten pounds, I'd guess—a deal.

Friday

I got the groceries and Louise picked them up on her way home from work. I loaded them into the trunk, her hunched over the steering wheel, craning her neck this way and that, expecting to see Sheldon lurking behind the carts. I got Muma some tensor bandages for her knee. She puts them on too tight and the stretch goes out of them after a while. It's not good for her circulation but try and tell her that. Louise says they might need someone full-time in the kitchen and do I want her to put my name in. Sure, why not? There's quite a few names in already, she says. Try anything, I say. Oranges are a decent price this time of year; I hate the way they stink up your fingers, that oil really gets in your pores but that's irrelevant, Muma and Louise like them so I got a couple dozen. Signed up for a beauty make-over at the drugstore—they do them three, four times a year. It only costs five bucks and you get a lot of free samples. Supposed to make you want to buy more.

Monday

Spent the afternoon at the mall. Tried on maybe twenty pairs of shoes. Drank six cups of coffee and smoked my brains out, me who was going to quit this week for sure. Boyd came home; him and Sheila had a big bust-up. He's been drinking because he's depressed about not finding another job and she says he's driving her crazy moping around the house, picking fights with her because he's hungover and feeling useless. He's sleeping on Muma's couch but if they don't make it up I'll have to share with Louise so he can have my room. Grey'll have a conniption. I told Boyd he's an ass to be drinking when he's got no money and no job. He's scared he'll lose his kids; put his head down on the kitchen table with the dirty dishes and bawled like a baby. Muma doesn't know what to do, she just looks at me like I should solve everybody's problems. Not to be iconoclastic but perhaps she hasn't noticed I'm not doing too well with my own? I guess I'll go see Sheila tomorrow. I got some candy for the kids, gum in a toothpaste tube. They like stuff like that. Chocolate bars, a six-pack for $1.99. Louise can put some in her glove compartment in case she gets stuck on the highway in a storm.


Wednesday

I don't know what came over me. I stopped in to pick up Muma's blood pressure pills, Louise's Zantac and a shirt for Grey for Valentine's and before I knew it I'd walked right into the travel agent's and started perusing the brochures. This woman came over, nice blue suit, pewter brooch, fake Hermes scarf, and before you could spit I was spinning her this tale about how me and my boyfriend are thinking of going south next month to get away from the slush and all. She gave me armloads of stuff and we talked packages and destination choices and Mexico vs. the Islands and narrowed it down to either St. Lucia or St. Kitts. We discussed sunblock and passports and Christ knows what all else. Lying isn't intrinsic with me, I haven't told a whopper like that since I was ten and told everybody at summer camp I had six sisters and eight brothers because I'd always wanted to come from a big family and figured they'd never find out any different. I couldn't stop, swear to God— it's like as long as I was talking to this woman it was real. I walked out the door and around the corner and dropped all the brochures into a trash can. Been depressed ever since. Must be this seasonal affective disorder they talk about. Get a grip, Sal. Go stand in a sunny window.

## Friday

It's true, you can't go back. Grey and I went out driving in his truck, round and round and finally out to the lake. It's paved now, the road around it is, and in the summer there are picnic tables and change rooms. There wasn't as much room as I remembered, and that jeezlus stick shift! Plus it was cold—seems to me we used to just radiate the heat, you couldn't see out the windows for steam. I started to laugh and then Grey got a crick in his back and started to holler. We ended up in his mother's garage with the lights off, standing up next to the garden tools. We're getting too old, I said after, as I was massaging the knot in his back, him leaning over the hood of the truck. If I thought I was too old for fucking I'd shoot myself, he said. That you, Grey? his mama called, snapping on the lights. We picked up the tools we'd knocked down, went in and had a cup of tea with her, trying to keep these inculpable looks on our faces. Then he drove me home. Your brother's a nice enough fella, he said, but I could learn to hate him. You just keep studying, I said, so you'll be ready when that job comes up.

## Monday

Sheila says she's had enough. She's moved in with her sister and she's filing for divorce. Boyd sits around in a Rangers T-shirt and Daddy's old pyjama bottoms eating Honey Nut Cheerios and milk out of Muma's stainless-steel mixing bowl. Watches talk shows. Sleeps twelve, fourteen hours at a stretch. Muma went to the doctor today for her blood pressure, he told her she's too tense and needs to learn to relax. Gave her a pamphlet on breathing exercises. Did you tell him about Boyd? I asked. No, she said, why would I do that? Boyd says he'll do the exercises with her. Louise says we should hide the salt shaker and not tell her where it is. Went to the mall after supper, got four pairs of one hundred percent cotton socks for $2.98. Masking tape at Biway, thirty-nine cents a roll, an inordinately good deal.

Wednesday

Nobody won the lottery yet, it's up to sixteen million. The line stretches past the Bata shoe store clear around the TD bank. Boyd asked me to pick him up ten dollars' worth. First money he's spent except for smokes since he came home. Grey got him on driving cab two mornings a week but he's saving to buy Kayla presents for her birthday. I'm thinking I better give Muma some extra for board until Boyd gets more work or moves out. I waited for an hour for the line-up to thin but more and more kept coming so finally I gave up and joined on. Sally looked pretty wasted, she's got a cold and had to keep stopping to blow her nose. I wonder what it must be like to take in all that money day after day and then take home your itsy paycheque. I guess you don't think about it being money. It'd drive you crazy. At least she's working full-time. Kayla will be four the end of the month. Or one. Seems like yesterday Boyd and me were getting coffee and honey crullers at the drive-thru at three in the morning, too excited to go straight home to bed after she was born. Got to Muma's at four and didn't he go get Kandace out of her crib, wake her up to tell her she'd got a new baby sister. Kandy cried and Muma scolded. Boyd just kept grinning, kissing everybody. It'll just kill him, losing those little girls. Plans to buy Kayla a bike for her birthday, a two-wheeler, and a new dress and one of those stuffed dogs with puppies in its belly. God only knows what all else. The man is an improvident fool.

Maureen Hull

Friday

Took Louise to the Clip Joint—she got her hair dyed because her therapist agreed she should go ahead if it made her feel more comfortable to disguise herself, just so she gets out and about. So now she's a sort of brunette with copper highlights, plus we picked out a pair of glasses with clear lenses. Yesterday evening she took every single thing in her closet and drawers that Sheldon had ever seen her wear, right down to her underpants, and put it all in garbage bags. Shoes she's hardly ever worn, her good leather coat, everything. The good stuff went to the Goodwill pick-up box, the rest got tossed in a dumpster behind the mall. Today she bought new stuff, different from anything she's ever worn. Nearly scorched the numbers off her Visa card. Then she took me to lunch, sat at a table by the big front window where everyone on the street could see her if they looked. I told her she should take dance lessons or a Tai Chi course, something to change the way she moves. She thought that was a good idea so I'm going to really push it. She needs something, is my guess, for when the novelty of the hair and clothes wears off. She started talking about moving west, says she's trained to do a heck of a lot more in a hospital than wash dishes and she'd have a better shot at a good job in Toronto or Edmonton or practically anyplace else. I don't know about that. Doesn't sound too shit hot anywhere, if you listen to the news every night. All the jobs gone to where it's warm and cheap, or squeezed and magically transformed into dividends in some CEO's pocket. Meanwhile I'm supposed to set up my own business and make blue widgets out of thin air and sell them to you and you're supposed to make red widgets out of spit and sell them to me. Then we'll both be just fine if you believe the politicians.

Monday

Took Muma on the bus to the dentist. Went to the mall while she was getting her bridge fixed. Batteries on sale so I bought a big pack and an extra flashlight. You never know when the power will go out this time of year. Saw Jeannine at the A&W with Brennon.

80

He's so cute. I never thought that much about having kids but I wouldn't mind one looks like Brennon. Grey's a good dad. He only gets him on Saturdays and has to have him back at bedtime, not that Jeannine's mean-minded or anything, she's just over-protective because Brennon was so sick when he was a baby. They rushed him to the hospital so many times that first year Grey says he lost count. He figures once Brennon's a little older and his lungs are bigger and tougher Jeannine will let him stay with Grey more often. He's a lot better than he used to be, though when he comes on Saturdays they have to shut the dog in the garage and vacuum the place from top to bottom. And absolutely incontrovertibly no smoking.


Wednesday

Louise is really pushing this going west business. She wants me to come with her for company and to share expenses. I don't know what to do. There's no work here. Part-time dribs and drabs, enough to squeeze the heart out of you and prolong the starvation process. Who'd keep an eye on Muma? And Boyd? Grey is the best guy I've come across in so long it's pathetic and I'd have to break up with him. I couldn't ask him to leave Brennon and I can't expect him to twiddle his thumbs, wait for me to come back who-knows-when. I started work right out of high school and been at it steady for ten years, right up until last year when the plant shut down for good. Now all I've got is EI for another few months and a couple of nights at the laundromat. Sore feet from walking to interviews because I can't afford the payments on the Corolla anymore. I can fill out job applications in my sleep but I'd be just as far ahead setting them afire for a little warmth. This isn't where I'm supposed to be by now. I'm supposed to have my own home, not half the extra bedroom at Muma's. I'm supposed to have a car, maybe a kid or two. A deck with a gas barbecue and something to cook on it. Somebody in Ontario won the lottery. I hope to hell they were poor and unemployed and have a big family they can share it with. Got pink and purple streamers, hats and horns for Kayla's party.

Friday

Forgot the balloons—sort of basic, you'd think I'd remember. Had to go back this morning for ice cream anyway. Kayla's birthday was actually yesterday but Boyd doesn't get the girls until today after school. Sheila's letting him keep them until Monday to make up for it. The VCR we gave Muma for Christmas three years ago is on the fritz but Grey's lending us his so we can rent some movies for the party. Disney stuff. The kids are sleeping in my old room so Boyd's back on the couch. I got Kayla new Barbie stuff and something for Kandy too. They've got it by the closetful but there's always something new they want. Sequins and spangles. Louise and me were just the same. Barbie—the family tradition. Jeannine's letting Grey bring Brennon over for a little while for cake and ice cream. The girls think he's some kind of doll, they're always wanting to take his clothes off or put them back on. Impudent or what. I got Brennon a present too. Why not, I'm thinking. I might not be here by the time his birthday comes around. Haven't told Grey or Muma yet.


Monday

I stayed to talk to Sheila after we took the girls back and asked her to keep an eye on Muma for me while I'm gone. She was furious but she will. We both know Boyd will drive Muma anywhere, jolly her spirits and play cards with her all day long, but he won't remember when to take her for her checkups and he can't do a thing in the house unless you aim him and say, Boyd, wash that floor, or Boyd, take out the garbage. Do anything if you tell him but Muma never would. That's half his problem, if you want to know. Sheila's mother died when she was twelve and she and Muma get along good so I know she'll take over for Louise and me. It's being around Boyd she doesn't want and she won't be able to avoid it. This is it, I told him. This is your last chance. Screw it up and you'll never get her or those kids back. I won't be here to tell you what to do either. It's grow-up time. He just sat there and cried. Daddy was six months in the hospital after his stroke before he died. One whole side frozen and he couldn't talk. Tears ran down the bad side of his face like a leaky tap.

Whenever he saw me the other eye would start and he'd sit there and cry for twenty minutes while I tried to make conversation. His birthday was February 29 too, same as Kayla. Quite a coincidence, two in one family. He would have been sixty-eight this year. Or seventeen, depending on how you count. Too young to die either way. I thought Muma'd be upset about me and Louise leaving. She's amazing, that one. Offered to give me some of Daddy's insurance money. You'll come back if you can't find something, she said. Daddy came and went a fair bit over the years, always hoping for that illusive good job that would let him sit back in his recliner in his own house every night after supper. She just pays the bills, cleans the house, makes a pan of fresh biscuits every day, and goes to church. Daddy got six months' retirement in before his stroke.

Wednesday

Inchoate—incomplete; only recently begun. Latin *inchoare* (to begin). Use that in a sentence, Sal. I am going west and my plans are inchoate.

Bought two suitcases, on sale at Zellers. Kelly green, my favourite. Bought new underwear too, in case we're in an accident— just kidding. And Grey's coming with us. The ambulance company he was hoping to get on with just laid off two guys been working there for fifteen years. Grey says not a hope in hell will he ever get a job there. We're staying an extra week so he can finish up his course; who knows, it might come in handy somewhere else. It would be stupid to quit this close to the end. I couldn't ask him to leave his little boy but he said himself there's nothing here and he can't do much for Brennon unless he gets some decent work. He's selling his truck so he can leave six months' support in the bank for Jeannine and have some to travel with. Louise is great; the more the merrier, she says, not to mention cheaper. We don't even know where we're going. Past Toronto anyway, further west. If we can't come up with one decent job in a city in two weeks we move on. Well, that's the plan, inchoate as hell. Bought new sunglasses so that afternoon sun blazing in from the west won't blind me. Going down the road at my age, for God's sake. That's what you do when you're nineteen, not pushing twenty-nine. Get a grip, Sal, I say when I start to shake. It's leap year. So take a flying leap.

# *Raspberry Jam*

One by one, I threw the jars as hard as I could. Glass smashed and sprayed against the porcelain; jam streaked, stained, gobbed like lumps of liver and heart onto the walls and slid to the floor. My arms were cut, my legs were slashed, there was jam blood and my blood everywhere. It was a temper tantrum. What else would you call it?

When Mother was seventy-four she moved to the valley to live with her cousin Thelma and Thelma's friend, Henrietta. They have an old farmhouse on the outskirts of a small town, and, by pooling their money, they are able to hire a housekeeper/nurse/companion. She, Deborah, comes six mornings a week, cleans, cooks, and doles out their various medications. She drives them to the doctor and, on Sundays, to church. It is ideal for Mother, who refuses to consider a home.

I'm ashamed to admit it but I don't want her in my house. The children have been gone these past five years, Ned is getting close to retirement, and I enjoy the stillness, the calm, uncluttered household I am finally able to maintain. Mother is a critical, bossy old woman. She sucks her teeth constantly.

Mother doesn't boss Thelma; Thelma won't have it. Hettie's hearing aid suffers power failure at frequent and unpredictable intervals. Deborah smiles, fingers her paycheque, and lets the fussing and picking flow around and past her.

I have tried to be a good daughter. I call every week. I never forget her birthday or Mother's Day and I put a lot of thought into her gifts. Every summer I spend an entire week in that house. I do try. I take her and her friends out on little trips, I let her order me about, and I never contradict her when she reminisces about Papa.

He was a deacon in the church, a Sunday school superintendent, a Mason and a member of the town council. He served as deputy mayor for five years. He ran a good Christian household. On Sundays we were permitted only to attend church, prepare the Sunday meal, go for walks and read the Bible. It was an exaggerated and smugly pious display for the rest of the congregation, who went swimming after church or to the movies in the evening. They were a pack of pagans whose devotion ended when they shook the pastor's hand on their way out of church. We, on the other hand, were suffocatingly righteous for the rest of the week.

Once, when I was twelve, I went swimming on a Sunday. Up until then I'd equated Papa's rules with church dogma, but it seems I'd been deceived. I had been staying with my best friend, and her father took us for a swim one hot August evening, after the late service. *Her* father was our minister. Papa was furious. It was exhilarating to watch him struggle to be civil when he was longing to tear a strip off the lot of us. I was careful not to provoke him; the tiniest smile would get me a whipping. Innocence plastered my face like cream on a Banbury tart.

It was hot when I drove to the valley last week. I dislike air conditioning. The flat mechanical roar and the cool impersonal temperature remind me of airports and airports make me nervous; I expect terrorists to boil out of the men's room, brandishing assault weapons and firing them at random. I opened the car windows and sped whenever possible to manufacture a breeze. I resisted the impulse to stop at every roadside stand on the way down. Two miles from Thelma's is MacLean's where everyone who knows buys new potatoes, corn, green and yellow beans, slender English cukes. The tomatoes are warm and sweet; the sunshine oozes out when you slice into them. I ate one, standing there under the awning, bending over so the juice wouldn't stain my blouse or drip on my sandalled feet.

I arrived in time to add cukes and tomatoes to the cold supper Hettie had laid out. We took our tea on the latticed porch, each one settled in her appointed white wicker chair, and traded news. Red geraniums in pots pulled the air in, close and privileged.

Hettie had fresh batteries and had been scavenging bits of this and that at the checkout at Sobey's, the dentist's office, the prescription counter at the drugstore. She knew it all: who was or wasn't having an affair, drinking too much, bankrupt, pregnant, abusing their children, beating their spouse. It is a continuing soap opera I am force-fed one week a year. Mother sends updates in her letters the other fifty-one weeks.

When I walk through the streets of that small valley town I am too embarrassed to look anyone in the eye. I know too much about them and their little sins and stumbles and I can't help wondering how much they know about me. Mother surely gossips about her children. It is pathetically easy to pull a confidence from her; she's very conscientious about returning value for value received. Anyone who tells her anything is rewarded with a tidbit from her own life (or anyone else's). She will dredge up some ancient embarrassing moment of one's life (my peculiar sleeping habits as a child, my first swimming lesson, the day I spilled tea on the minister's wife). She will freshen it up, add something a little more current and offer it as a politeness.

My parents and their peers believed that all children could and should swim. Tossing them into deep water was simply a way to kick-start dormant ability. The survival instinct propelled the child, kicking and sputtering, to the shore. From that point on, one simply required practice. I've never forgotten the terror as I flailed my way to safety. I was six that summer and small for my age. As they laughed and applauded I stumbled across the rocky shore and ran into the woods, howling with fear and rage. I begged, grovelled to the fates to send some avenging sea monster to snatch all the adults,

Papa in particular, by the ankles and drag them into the lake to drown. Eventually I did learn to swim and to enjoy it but I don't believe I've ever forgiven them. My children took properly supervised Red Cross lessons at a pool and won any number of swimming trophies. Quite often on a Sunday.

It is curious that Papa never acknowledged the contradiction between his Victorian fundamentalist pose and his grand secular passion. He loved to sing and he loved to do it onstage in an elaborate costume. Every year he performed with a local drama club. They were keen on operettas, and if they chose a Gilbert and Sullivan and he didn't get a leading role he made our lives miserable with his pouting. Fortunately, he almost always got a substantial part. His favourite role, and he played it many times, was Captain Corcoran of the H.M.S. Pinafore. Papa had a passable voice, a bit fruity and bombastic, but that sort of thing was much admired then. He was never so happy or amiable as when he was being praised for his singing. No compliment could be too extravagant; he swallowed them whole and was ravenous for more. Despite his hearty disclaimers he believed every sycophantic phrase. He became, for all intents and purposes, drunk with praise.

Mother never went onstage. She had quite a good voice but said she was not comfortable under the gaze of an audience. Papa did not encourage her; he needed her to play piano accompaniment while he practised and it took a great deal of her time to construct his costumes. He had two for *Pinafore*, both elaborate pseudo–Royal Navy pushed beyond the bounds of good taste. One of my jobs was to polish the innumerable brass or silver buttons before each show. They had to gleam like pirate treasure.

Mother must have stitched a small fortune in gold and silver braid onto the costumes. The braids came in a large box from Malabar's in Toronto, as did the ostrich feathers he wore in his cocked hats. Before each season I would take the feathers from their tissue-paper storage and soak them in warm water with a sprinkle of soap flakes and a touch of blueing. When rinsed, they looked dreadful, a handful of sticks with sodden hair along their length. Mother would smartly tap the spines against the back of a chair, over and over. Gradually they would begin to dry; bit by bit they would fluff out until they were reborn as magnificent billowing plumes.

Papa liked to play captains of ships, generals, colonels in the cavalry, characters of exaggerated dignity and high moral tone. As he swept across the stage I could sometimes forget it was Papa under all the gilt and lofty integrity. He was really quite a good actor. When I tried to tell Mother what he was really like, she wouldn't believe me.


I thought I was the only one. Of course, now I know better; it's in every newscast, in every magazine. There are books and books. People actually go on television and tell their stories to total strangers. So many secrets shaking loose. So many houses all around my childhood, houses in towns, villages and cities where men and sometimes women behaved despicably to small children. Same secret, different details.

They make me so cross with their statistics. One in four, they say. One in seven, one in three. How on earth could they know such a thing? Do they send out questionnaires, for pity's sake? Do phone surveys? What about the ones who never tell? The ones who, if asked, lie? The ones like me who think it's nobody's business but mine?

I sometimes wonder—who else in the junior choir, the Mission Circle, the Girl Guides? The one who got in trouble and disappeared for a year? The one who married at nineteen, had five children in a row and ate herself to two hundred and sixty pounds by her thirtieth birthday? The one who told lies, pinched, and stole dimes from the collection plate? The exemplary one—you'd never guess it's her. She's a registered nurse, she married a successful businessman, but she's still afraid of the dark; hysteria threads her prayers. I'm guessing, true, when I look in women's eyes—as they pour the tea or roll coins from the collection plate. Sometimes it's a stranger gazing past me in a coffee shop. I snag the vacant stare of a bundled, parcelled woman and I think I can see it. I think I can see the thing in the mirror, the hole behind the eyes, the place where things have died and are lost forever. I understand everyone goes to therapy, now. I never have.

Why would I want to talk about it? I manage not to think about it most of the time. Why would I want to talk to a stranger? I don't like strangers near me.

The last few years Mother embraces me when I arrive for my visit. She's probably read an article about it in the *Reader's Digest*—"Connect with Your Adult Children," or some such thing. She'd stand on her head if the *Reader's Digest* recommended it.

Mother has always had raspberry canes in the backyard. When we moved, each time to a bigger house to keep pace with Papa's inflated status, she dug the canes up and moved them with us. In two years' time they would be producing berries by the quart. We ate them until we got hives and then we made jam with the rest. There was always too much jam. There was always more than enough to tide us over that first year after a move, before the canes would begin to fruit again. When Mother moved in with Thelma she had me dig up her canes and bring them along. We ripped up Thelma's few neglected plants (an inferior variety, according to Mother) and threw them in the burning barrel.

Unpicked berries will get fat and sticky on the canes, turn wine-red, watery and intensely sweet; summer rain will smash them to paste on the ground. The wasps hum and swarm around the bushes constantly, crawling over the berries, rasping at the drupes, opening them up to mould and rot. The wasps are greedy, drunk and territorial. You must move among them slowly and carefully.

I knew when he was coming. I could sense his silent approach in the hall outside the bedroom and I would explode from whatever dream held me to a heart-pounding alert. I could feel the smooth brass doorknob against his palm, could hear the slide of his skin against his nightclothes, could see the black walls shifting to grey rectangles as the door opened. He liked long hair; he wouldn't let Mother cut ours. He'd reach down and pull one long braid and I would be trapped at the end of it. Not since I was very small had he needed to cover my mouth to smother any noise I might make. He'd pull that braid out of bed, into the hall and down to the spare room at the back of the house. Here were all the sick plants; it was a little greenhouse infirmary with big windows for the ones that needed extra sun and nourishment and attention. Moist earth and vegetable rot. The slow tick of the clock in the hall. I told myself stories as he masturbated into my hand or against my belly. He would leave me there in the dark and I would wait until I was sure it was safe to tiptoe to the bathroom, to wash in the dark, the tap a slow trickle so no one would hear. Safe to slide back into my bed with its flinty sheets and basalt mattress. In the morning I tortured her plants. Shook them out of their pots and jammed them back in again. Knocked them over and blamed the cat. Spit on them. Poured rubbing alcohol into their saucers. They usually died. She never knew why.

At the end of my visits, Mother parcels up a box of her raspberry jam. Ned watches his weight and I dislike raspberry jam but she always insists on giving me a case.

"Don't forget to return the bottles for next year!" she says, but I never do. Once I managed to "forget" them; twice I gave them to the food bank. Three years ago they were stolen from the back seat when I stopped for coffee. I leave the doors unlocked now when I stop, but no one's wanted them since.

I was late getting away; Mother was fussing and bossing more than usual. I could feel the headache beginning between my shoulder blades, moving up the back of my neck. Halfway home I had to stop at a motel; the pain in my head made it impossible to drive. The pavement rippled and shook; it broke the afternoon light into needles and drove them into my brain. I took a room and lay down on the bed, pills and water in hand. The line of sunlight marking the bottom of the drapes slowly faded. By the time my head eased it was late evening so I decided to stay and start fresh in the morning. But I was unable to sleep, even with the light on, the door locked, and the bureau pulled over against it.

As I child I sometimes tried to sleep under my bed or made nests in the closet after my parents thought I was asleep. If Mother found me she would chase me back to bed. Sometimes discomfort drove me out. I'd get into bed with my sister, hoping there would be safety in numbers. But the bed was too narrow; we kicked; it was impossible. There was never a safe place to rest. I never said no out loud. I believed if I did, he would kill me. All the years of my childhood, I was so tired. I could never find a safe place to sleep.

Finally I got up and went out to the car to get my new book. The previous morning I had taken the old ladies downtown to the hairdresser and then to the bookstore. There I'd bought myself a new hardcover copy of *The Horse's Mouth* by Joyce Cary. I first read it in university and have reread it every three or four years since. It is my favourite of the thousands of novels I've read and my copy had become somewhat worn. I almost never buy hardcover: I require paperbacks that slip easily into my pocket or purse so I am never without something to read.

*The Horse's Mouth* was a present to myself—for being a good daughter, for holding my tongue, I suppose. Gully Jimson, that scruffy old man—wickedly funny, and so passionate—has always entranced me. He cares nothing for the law, for public opinion, for rules and regulations; he will do anything—lie, cheat, steal—to get his hands on some paint and a surface to put it on. In the pursuit of his vision, always slightly ahead of his grasp, it seems, he is more alive than anyone I've met in real life.

Thelma wanted westerns; Mother went for the Harlequins. Hettie browsed the self-help section.

"You're never so old as to be perfect," said Hettie. "It never hurts to try to improve yourself."

"Tai Chi," sniffed Mother, "that's the latest. Goes out in the backyard and waves her arms around to music."

"Tai Chi is excellent exercise for the body and mind," I defended Hettie.

"If she wants to improve her body she could help me weed," said Mother, "and if she wants to improve her mind she should read the Bible for an hour every day. I do." She slapped *Haven of Hope*, *Ribbons for Rowena* and *Love's Last Breath* into my basket.

I checked carefully but there was no one in the parking lot, or on the street, so I unlocked the car and reached into the back seat. She'd put her box on top of my new book. Somehow several of the jars had cracked and leaked. The jam had spoiled the first dozen chapters, glued the crisp white sheets together. I could have cried. I took the book inside and carefully sponged each page, then set it upright and fanned it open to dry. The pages were stained pink, a fever spreading upward. They would dry wrinkled, buckled, would never lie flat and perfect again. She'd ruined my book with her stupid jam. I went back out to the car.

I carried the box into the bathroom to dispose of the broken jars. Three were cracked and jam was dripping onto the floor. I picked out the loose shards and dropped them into the wastebasket, then began to rinse off the nine unbroken ones, placing each carefully on the edge of the bathtub. When they were lined up in a row I reached for a towel to dry them, hesitated, then pushed one over into the tub. It landed with a dull crack and split in two. The jam glistened in the bare bright light. I picked up a second jar and dropped it from shoulder height. Much better. I threw the rest, one at a time, smashing them against the walls, the tub and the floor as hard as I could. Furious flowers bloomed everywhere; the pain in my head splashed all around the room. Flying shards of glass cut my arms and slashed my legs. Jam and blood ran down the tiles and pooled at my feet.

When I begged her to save me from him, she screamed at me that I was a liar. She hit me across the face with the big wooden spoon she was using to stir the jam. The burn from the hot sticky mess healed and eventually faded, but still, when I am very upset, a red mark appears on my cheek.

Afterwards, I scrubbed the bathroom clean again. The pieces of jam flesh slithered down the drain, breaking into smaller and smaller lumps to get past the hair trap. I put the broken glass back in the box, tied it shut with my pantyhose and left it in the garbage. I washed my arms and legs with cold water until they stopped bleeding and then crawled back to bed. I was exhausted. I fell asleep immediately and didn't wake until the maid knocked on the door the next day.

"It's past noon, dear," she apologized. "I got to clean your room." She stood just outside the door on the narrow concrete walk that ran along in front of all the units. One hand jingled her keys; the other rested on the cart that held her vacuum, buckets, cleaners and rags. Behind her the day was as fresh and pretty as I'd seen all summer.

# Boy in the Pear Tree

He sat in the upper branches of the pear tree, motionless. I thought he had come to steal the pears. The children from the neighbourhood take fruit from the garden, although I hand it out by the bushel. It's the adventure of a raid that appeals to them. I pretended not to see him, so I wouldn't spoil his game, and picked a handful of broccoli shoots for supper. I returned to the house and caught a glimpse of his features through the back window but I didn't recognize his face. When he slid out of the branches and over the fence the leaves of the pear tree scarcely moved.

After that I noticed him often, always in hiding, never with the other children. He took nothing. He came quietly, climbed the pear tree and sat in silence, meditating or watching—I wasn't sure which. I didn't mention it to my wife. Alice doesn't approve of the children helping themselves to the fruit; she doesn't like them running in and out of the garden. I thought she might chase him away, or challenge him and make him explain himself; she likes people to explain themselves. Alice only goes into the garden to cut flowers. She doesn't dawdle. She decapitates them briskly and arranges them in two copper bowls in the front hall. She would never notice a silent child in the branches above her head. So I kept quiet. I thought, he *needs* to sit in that tree. If I frighten him, he might not be able to find another.

The snow came in November before the leaves had all fallen. I didn't see him again until late in January; he was across the street, watching me shovel the front drive. I waved and he lifted a red mitten a few inches, then jammed it in his pocket and marched quickly away. Winter lurched on, stalled, moved again. April arrived and the cold wet ground grew steamy in the mild spring air.

I was with Bud Morris, taking a shortcut through the park on our way home from the Legion, where we'd taken a pounding at the dartboard. The boy was in what they call a half-pipe, one of those things they put up to keep the skateboarders off the streets and out of the parking lots—like a big pipe cut lengthwise and laid on its side. He and some others were rolling back and forth like marbles in a bowl; when they reached the rim they'd twist and flip around in mid-air, then roar down and back up to the opposite edge. These kids—they walk along, all slumped over with big feet and gawky elbows—put them on a skateboard and they turn into angels, graceful and full of power.

"Who's that kid?" I asked Bud, pointing. "The one in the green sweatshirt."

He looked at me, astonished, then embarrassed when he saw that I really didn't know.

"That's Maryanne's boy."

I didn't have another word to say all the way home.

He looks to be about eight or nine but I know exactly how old he is. He's eleven, small and wiry. He has his mother's build and her dark straight hair. I can't see anything of his father at all. The eyes are his grandmother's, although at first I missed the resemblance. They hold mistrust and innocence, constantly shifting; they change colour with his emotions. Alice's eyes have long since fossilized in her head, the colours muddled to the grey stone of petrified tree stumps.


I was forty-seven when John was born; Alice was forty-four. We'd pretty much given up all hope of having children. I wasn't against adoption but Alice was fierce about having her own. When John surprised us she didn't want to share him with anyone. In the middle of the night I would find her leaning over his bed, watching. She looked as if she were trying to breathe for him. She wanted him to be perfect. She wanted to do everything perfectly for him. She spent hours fussing over his clothes, reading to him, doing things, constantly doing things for him. She took him to the doctor every three months; she carefully screened his playmates. If he hadn't been such a good-tempered little fellow he would have been completely spoiled. It wasn't until he was about six or seven that he became my boy. Tried to walk like me, had to have a hat like mine. Wanted to follow me everywhere. Alice didn't like that. He should have been twins; we pulled him apart.

When he and Maryanne, both in high school, came to tell us that Maryanne was pregnant and they wanted to be married, Alice said terrible things. She drove them off with cruel words. She called the girl wicked names. I didn't know what to do; I didn't want him to cut off his future. He was meant to go to college, to be an engineer. So I didn't do anything.

John continued to live at home and he stayed in school. The girl broke up with him. He told me that when he tried to see her she refused to speak to him. He began to drink. I could smell it on him, but he denied it and his mother wouldn't listen to me. Maryanne had her boy and then she left town. I sent her some money. Alice said good riddance. John drank a quart of rum and drove into an overpass on a clear Tuesday night in December.

It was 1:15 a.m. when the RCMP knocked at the door. We both went to the hospital but it was too late. When they told Alice that John had been drunk, her face closed up like a cellar door. After we left the hospital I took her back to the house and then went for a long drive. I couldn't make myself go home although I knew I should. When I finally returned it was six in the morning. She was ironing his best shirt. She had his suit and her favourite tie out, ready to go to the cleaners the minute they opened. His shoes sat on top of the refrigerator, polished so I could see my face in them as I walked into the kitchen.

"They won't want his shoes," I said, but she ignored me and I did not speak again.

We took his things, his perfectly ironed silk shirt, his immaculately cleaned and pressed suit and tie, and his gleaming shoes, to the funeral home. Then we buried him. I thought the pain would ease as the years went by, but it never did.

I have birdhouses in my backyard. I first built them next to the fence where the trees are thick. Then, each year, I moved them a little closer until now they're on posts directly outside my dining-room window. The birds come back, year after year, and I can sit and have my coffee and watch the parents jam bugs down the little ones' throats. When they first sidle out to look at the world and think about flying, I'm there to wish them luck and cheer them on.

It took all spring and most of the summer but by the end of August I could sit under the pear tree and read the paper while he sat above me. By September he'd toss me down a pear to eat. By October he was helping me rake the leaves.

"Who is that kid?" demanded Alice. "You want to watch those tools or he'll steal them."

"Just a kid," I said. "He doesn't steal."

We began to talk a little, about this and that. I hired him to help pile and bag the leaves when they got too thick.

"My mom says your wife is an old witch," he said one day as we were putting the rakes back in the shed.

When I didn't answer he looked defiant, then frightened. What could I say? She's been disappointed. Shamed by the son who fell so short of her dreams. She'll soften towards you, eventually. She has something for you—some gift of affection that only you can coax out of her chilly soul.

"She was very unkind to your mother," I said at last. His shoulder blades were a ridge of bone; he held his body tensed and ready to fling free. Something more needed to be said, but I'm not good with words. I think a lot about things and I can write a fairly decent letter but as for talking—I've never been able to gather the right words until it's too late. I cleared my throat and tried to think.

He edged towards the gate, his fingers twitching and picking the paint from the boards. I jammed my own into my pockets.

"I've been thinking," I said, for lack of anything better, "of building some new birdhouses. The ones I have are pretty old—the bottoms rot after a while—and I thought I'd make some extras for the church. To sell at their flea market, to raise money, you know? I was wondering if you'd give me a hand with them?"

"I don't know how." He stopped peeling paint, his fingers flexing, making fists, then flicking away air.

"I don't need a carpenter. Just someone to hold the other end of the board and hand me nails. An assistant. I'm going to start tomorrow and I'll probably be at it for the next couple of weeks. I should warn you, I don't pay much."

"No kidding." The corner of his mouth quirked and I imagined feathers settling, ever so slightly.

"You could come by after school—if your mother doesn't mind."

"She don't mind." His shoulder blades eased back down. "I got to go now."

"I'll see you tomorrow, then."

"See ya."

He drifted up the street, hands in his pockets, big sneaker feet scuffing the leaves. Suddenly he lunged high into the air, grabbed a handful of red maple leaves and tore them loose. Then he was running, jumping, zig-zagging back and forth across the street, twisting, grabbing, scattering yellow, brown, red and orange pennants to the ground; counting coup on every tree until he swerved around the corner and out of my sight.

I pulled my watch out of my pocket and examined its lovely finger-worn sheen. My father's name is engraved inside the lid, John Farrell, and under it, my own, William John Farrell. Below that, empty space.

It's a greedy, aching thing to imagine myself giving this watch to the boy. I have no right to give, or to take. No rights at all. Just now there are more practical things to think about. I need a new blade for the jigsaw and a pound of finish nails. We'll need primer and paint. I'd better make a list.

# *Livy*

Livy braces herself, one foot against each muddy ditch wall, leans over and stirs the turgid water with a stick. A beetle on a leaf floats past. She pushes him under. Earthworms, flushed by last night's rain, make question marks and commas. She flips them into the water and they spiral to the bottom. Her left foot slips; she jams it harder against the wall and leans on the stick. When it snaps she lands hands down; silted muddy water splashes into her mouth. She spits. Again and again. Dead worms roll against her fingers.

"Gross!" she shrieks and flings herself up onto the warm sidewalk. She yanks off her muddy shoes, shoves her socks into the toes, wipes her feet and hands on some grass, and walks home, dangling her shoes from a broken alder branch. She drops them on the back step and explains to her aunt, "I fell in a ditch."

"You look it," says Barbara. She is peeling potatoes in the sink, a dishtowel draped over her shoulder. There is mud on the seat of her work pants. "Get in the tub right now. Company coming."

"A whole bath? How about I just wash my feet?"

"A whole bath. And put those clothes in the washer."

"Can I have milk and cookies first?"

"No."

Half an hour later Livy is reasonably clean, snacking at the kitchen table. "Stop feeding that dog cookies," says Barbara. "They rot his teeth and make him fart."

"Yes, Baba."

"Don't you want to know who's coming?"

"Denise with my birthday present."

"Denise and her new husband."

"Denise got a husband? But I wasn't there! You never told me!"

"Didn't tell me until this morning. Called up to say they got married and she was bringing him along. That Bill she talks about."

"I could of been a junior bridesmaid like Carolyn with a long dress and flowers in my hair. She's mean not to let me be a bridesmaid. She's the meanest sister in the world."

"It's her wedding. When you get married you can do it your way."

"Well, I'm not letting her be *my* bridesmaid. Bimbo'll be my bridesmaid." Livy pulls the dishtowel from Barbara's shoulder and drapes it over the dog's head. "Look, Baba. Bimbo's getting married."

Denise and Bill arrive late. Denise had dozed off and Bill had taken a wrong turn. They eat warmed-over suppers while Barbara pours coffee and smiles and nods. Livy examines everyone through chunks of lime jello and picks at the corners of the presents she isn't to open until tomorrow. Barbara has put on a dress, and it isn't even Sunday. Denise seems to be taking up a lot of space; she laughs and chatters and the overhead light reflects from her eyes, her teeth, her sparkling rings. Livy is temporarily dazzled into silence. Her birthday has been eclipsed by Denise's sudden marriage and Bill's introduction into the family. Livy doesn't mind. Not as long as she is being entertained. Sparkly Denise is interesting enough for one whole evening, and she's barely begun to watch Bill. He sits at the end of the table, a neat, steady eater who doesn't let go of his knife and fork until he's completely finished. He doesn't talk much. Denise probably doesn't let him, thinks Livy. She spoons up a fresh jello lens and puts him behind it. The hair on his head is slipping backwards but his moustache is a bristly brown caterpillar. He pets it regularly, smoothing it down to his upper lip, coaxing the hairs to lie together neatly. When the jello is finished, Livy takes Bimbo outside to run and run until their brains empty out and they fall down on the lawn. Livy is a starfish on her back; Bimbo pants beside her. Her head fills with royal blue sky and a slice of silver moon. Sent to bed, she falls asleep with the smell of cut grass on her palms and dreams she wears stars on all her fingers, presents from Denise.

When Denise and Bill have settled into their room, Barbara makes her rounds. Once around the yard, a pause at the chicken coop to check the latch. She finds Livy's muddy sneakers and puts them on the washing machine for the morning. She locks the doors and turns out the lights behind her as she goes upstairs. Livy is muttering in her sleep. "Those are mine!" she says.

Barbara reads in bed for twenty minutes, then folds the magazine shut and stares at the ceiling. Overdue for a fresh coat of paint, she thinks. Hasn't seen a brush since before the girls came. She lies quietly, remembering Livy's birth and Cassie's death.

At the end, it seemed as though her sister had burned down to fine grey ash. Barbara thought it was Cassie's skin, loose and flaking, that had kept the particles of powdered bone and dried flesh from drifting away. She'd sat in a chair by the window, trying to stay awake in case Cassie needed her. Occasionally, she drifted off. That last night the plastic bite of the chair on the backs of her knees, and the silence, woke her. When she leaned over to look, Cassie's eyes were matte black, the glaze of drugs rubbed off. Barbara held her sister's hand for a while, making a private space before stirring up the brisk trot of the night nurse, the jangle and whisk of bed curtains, and the rumble of stretcher wheels along the tiled corridor.

Denise went into labour during the funeral service, and Barbara spent the afternoon and evening back at the hospital, hot and weary in her one black dress. Denise was locked onto Barbara's arm, alternately weeping and screeching. Cassie was buried with none of her family at the graveside.

Denise's baby, Olivia Cassandra, was red fists, spiky black hair and howls. Barbara brought them both home and put them to bed, her poor sister Cassie's girls, she told nosy neighbours. She let drop that Cassie had fought off her cancer long enough to allow the baby to be born. It was the sort of miracle people were grateful to hear, shaking their heads in admiration for the tenacity and power of maternal love.

"No need to make your life any more complicated than it already is," she'd told Denise. Denise stayed in bed, pulled the covers over her head and wept for her mother whenever the baby wailed.

There had been days Barbara'd wanted to slap Denise senseless, stuff the baby into a closet and then drink a bottle of Scotch. Instead, she'd driven Denise once a week to a therapist in the city, bought herself and Denise earplugs for when Livy's colic was particularly bad, and spent a lot of time cleaning out the chicken coop. The mungy air of the coop—wet, half-rotted straw, chicken shit and feathers—seemed to steady her. Some weeks she'd cleaned it daily.

By late spring, Denise had stopped weeping and was set to graduate from high school. Livy had quit screaming and was dispensing sloppy, three-toothed grins. The chickens had pretty much given up laying, their nerves shot to hell.

In June Barbara took the girls to the city to put flowers on Cassie's grave. She bought the baby a doll and a pair of red rubber boots for her first birthday. Livy, barely walking, loved the boots, kicked and yelled when they tried to take them off her feet at bed-time.

"Soon as I graduate from secretarial school and get a job I'll take her off your hands," said Denise.

For Livy's third birthday, Denise brought a beautiful, handmade doll, dressed in a Victorian nightgown and mob cap, heavy with lace and ribbon. The long-lashed eyes were embroidered shut. Livy wouldn't touch it.

"Don't you like her?" Denise was a little put out. She was proud of her first job, the fact that she could buy Livy an expensive present.

"Shhhh." Livy tiptoed past the doll. "Baby sleeping."

"You take her now," said Barbara, "you'll have to start toilet training all over. The change will upset her."

"Shouldn't she already be toilet trained?"

"You can't rush Livy. Take her if you want. I'm just telling you."

Denise thought Livy was spoiled. "She won't mind me. She never does what I tell her."

Barbara laughed so hard she sloshed coffee onto the blue-checked tablecloth.

Denise frowned at her. "You encourage her to sauce me. You're as bad as she is."

The house was full of Livy—her possessions and babble spilling from one room to the next. Denise felt quite flattened, as if she had to paper herself against the walls to make room for whirligig Livy and solid Barbara. She flapped in the wake of their to and fro-ing. As she drove back to the city she felt herself slowly regain substance. By the time she opened her apartment door she had weight and colour. She pummelled a few throw cushions. Straightened the magazines on her coffee table.

The following year, Denise phoned Barbara to say she'd be late and to start the party without her. Livy fell asleep shortly after ten o'clock, and Barbara began cleaning up. Her next-door neighbour, Marda, came over with a bottle of vodka.

"Stuff's like glue," she said, helping to scrape pink icing from the linoleum. By eleven the garbage can was overflowing with streamers, balloon skins and crumpled party hats with snapped elastics. The dishes had been washed and it was finally safe to walk on the floor. Barbara was mixing the third round of vodka and tonic, Marda was embroidering local gossip when Denise pushed open the kitchen door.

"I can hear you cackling from the yard. You sound like demented hyenas. Lord"—she picked up the bottle—"you haven't drunk all this vodka yourselves?"

"Hi, Denise. Plenty left for you."

"Where's the baby?"

"Asleep hours ago. I can't keep her up all night waiting for you to show."

"I couldn't get away. Should you be drinking like this when she's asleep?"

"Would you rather I drank like this while she's awake? Don't you lecture me, Denise; you don't like how I'm raising her, you can take her in the morning."

"Well, maybe I'll do just that!"

"Then do it and quit talking about it."

Denise swished the vodka around in the bottle, then reached in the cupboard for a glass and made herself a large one.

"Barb, I can't take her with me. My landlord doesn't allow kids. I'm sorry I bitched at you; I just feel bad about missing her party."

"Any time you think I'm not raising her right—"

"No, no. I do. She's fine, she's happy. I'm sorry."

"All right then."

"Next year, before she starts school. I have to find another place first."

Denise took Livy to Disney World for her fifth birthday. "God, I'm beat! I had to watch her every second. I don't know how you stand it. She'll talk to anybody!"

Livy had a suitcase full of junk to show Barbara: Mickey Mouse ears, stuffed toys, fluorescent T-shirts, a pet land crab that had expired on the trip home and was beginning to stink.

Barbara's present squirmed out of his basket behind the stove and licked Livy's chin. "Ick!" said Livy, and licked him back.

"She can't take that dog when she comes to live with me," whispered Denise.

"When might that be?" asked Barbara.

"I don't know. Soon."

Barbara enrolled Livy in the elementary school a half mile up the road and bought her new clothes for September. She had to tie the pup to the porch the first six months to keep him from following Livy to class.

Livy liked school. Numbers, lunch, recess and art were her favourites. She made black witches with green faces, red sleighs with purple presents, pink valentines on paper lace. In June they made cards for Father's Day. On hers Livy drew the farm: the house, the sheep barn, the apple tree. She put Bimbo in his doghouse and coloured him a big dish full of double-stuff Oreos. She put sheep under the apple tree and drew apples falling on their stupid heads. She drew herself on the porch, waving. She brought the card home to Barbara.

"Where's my father?"

"He's dead. You know that."

"Yes, but where's he dead?"

"I don't know. Somewhere in Alberta. He left your mother before you were born."

"Why?"

"I don't know. Sometimes people don't get along."

"I'd have gotten along with him. He would of come back. If he hadn't of died. He would of come back for me."

"Would *have*."

"Would *have* come back for me. For me!"

"He wouldn't have been able to stay away."

Barbara rolls over and turns off the lamp. Fathers, she thinks. Livy has been talking about fathers lately. When she was very small, men frightened her, but the older she gets the more she likes them and the more she thinks they should have one.

"Baba," she'd said, just the other week, "let's you get married."

"What!"

"Let's get you a husband."

"Not me, thank you very much."

"Don't you want to wear a bride dress and have somebody to help shovel?"

"No. Men are worse to clean up after than sheep."

"But Baba, I don't have a father and all my friends do."

"You have me and Denise and the farm and Bimbo. Not everybody gets everything. Didn't you say Carolyn's father wouldn't let her have a dog?"

"Yes. He's mean."

"He's not mean. You just can't always have everything you want."

"It's not fair."

"Life is not fair. It's interesting but it's not fair."

Bill seems a nice-enough fellow. Not that you can tell much after one evening. She tucks the covers under her chin and shuts her eyes. I have to talk to Denise tomorrow, she thinks. I won't put it off any longer.


The next morning Barbara makes birthday waffles with strawberries and whipped cream. Denise does the dishes and Barbara leaves for town to pick up four of Livy's friends.

"Go outside now, while I decorate," Denise tells Livy.

Bill sits on the back steps, big feet spread out on the ground for balance. He is whittling, something he remembers from summers with his grandfather and that he feels is appropriate here. He is trying to carve a dagger, the only thing he ever wanted to make as a kid, although his grandfather carved animals—dogs curled up asleep, pigs with wrinkled snouts and curly tails, cows with tiny bags and teats—and would have taught Bill if he'd been interested. His sister-in-law has most of those animals now, "folk art" in a glass cabinet in her dining room. Bill is trying to think of a way to get Livy to come to him. He thinks it would be better if she approached him first but she throws sticks for Bimbo, hangs upside down from branches and ignores him. He isn't sure if this means she doesn't like him or she's just shy. He wants to be friends; even, if they get along, to try to be a father—if that's what Denise wants. He carves a row of X's around the hilt, folds the knife shut and puts it in his shirt pocket, then throws the dagger for Bimbo to catch. The dog leaps, twists in mid-air and snatches it with his teeth. Takes it to Livy. She slowly brings it back to the steps.

"Can I have it?"

"Sure. I made it for you. Bimbo's pretty fast. He could catch knives in a circus."

Livy stares at him but doesn't reply. It feels like she's peeling his skin off to count his bones. "So why do you call him Bimbo? Isn't it supposed to be Bingo?"

Livy rolls her eyes. "No way! His name is Bimbo, from the REAL song about Bimbo." She begins to sing, enthusiastically.

Denise leans over the porch railing to watch.

"It's from an old Jim Reeves album. We had to play it half a dozen times every night to get Livy to sleep when she was a baby. It got so worn Barb finally threw it out."

"Bimbo can't be in a circus," says Livy, leaning against Bill's knee and plucking the knife from his shirt pocket. "He'd die if he couldn't live on the farm with me and Baba."

"Put that knife back, Livy. It's sharp and you didn't ask." Denise is quick to scold.

Bill takes the knife from Livy and repositions it in her hand. "You might as well learn how to handle it properly. Want to make your own dagger?"

"I want to make a sword."

When Barbara returns there are wood chips all over the backyard. Livy has two bandages and Bill has three. The sword is crude in shape but has a hilt knife-scored and crayon-coloured to suggest jewels. Livy and her friends play knights-in-armour with the sword and dagger while Denise puts the hot dogs on the barbecue and Bill rests on the couch.

"She likes me," he says.

After the hot dogs, cake, ice cream and presents, Bill takes the kids to a movie. Barbara brings two cups of tea to the table.

"Does Bill know Livy's yours?"

"Yes. She likes him, don't you think?"

"Are you taking her?"

"Well, we're buying a house, a lovely house, three bedrooms, but we can't move in until November. I'm pregnant, Barb, and with the baby due in January we thought it would be too much all at once. We thought the summer after, when we're settled. If you'd just keep her another year?"

Barbara gets up, goes to a desk in the corner under the stairs and yanks open the bottom drawer. She pulls out a large brown envelope and lays it on the table in front of Denise.

"What's this?"

"Adoption papers. I had them drawn up a couple of years back. This can't go on, Denise. I'm too old to be jerked around anymore."

Denise opens her mouth but no sound comes out.

"I'm not your babysitter, Denise. You flip in and out of here, me never knowing when you'll decide to take her away. Give her to me legal or take her now."

Denise looks as if she's been slapped.

"I'm going to weed the beets. You talk this over with Bill and let me know by tomorrow dinnertime." Barbara closes the screen door quietly. Her footsteps fade across the yard. The kitchen is silent except for the crinkle of paper as Denise pulls out the long white sheets. She wants to lay her head on the table and cry. She wants Bill to come back from town and make everything all right. She pinches her arms, hard, and begins to read.


Monday morning Barbara and Denise sit in Barbara's car on the shady side of Provost Street. The long brown envelope with the signed papers rests on the seat behind them. It's hot for June, hot enough to be August. The new leaves on the red maples are scorched on the edges. Barbara watches Junior Maynes pick half-eaten doughnuts out of the garbage in front of Tim Horton's.

"Remember Mr. Maynes? He used to be the janitor at the town hall. Before they joined us on to St. Alice and got rid of the mayor and half the town councillors. Useless bunch they were."

"I don't want her to think I abandoned her. I don't want her to hate me." Denise twists the top button on her dress. "We'll have to tell her sometime and then she'll hate me."

"She'll be mad at the pair of us when she finds we've been lying to her," says Barbara. "She'll get over it. Here." She hands Denise a small blue envelope. "You can use this to help buy that house of yours."

Denise opens the envelope, looks at the cheque. "Barb, you can't afford this!"

"It's your college money. You know I'd have sent you, but you didn't want to go."

"Can you see me in college?" Denise elbows her aunt and tries to chuckle. "But you should keep it for Livy. She'll go."

"She'll run the damn place. Don't worry, there'll be enough for her. I started a bank account in her name when she was born. I add to it every year—you know me, get two pennies, save one. I'd have given this to you anyway; I just hung onto it in case you changed your mind about school. And then, I didn't want you to think I was trying to buy Livy or anything. So I held back until we'd settled things."

"You know you railroaded me, you wicked old woman."

"I made you stop fooling yourself."

"I love her, Barb, but—she scares me a little. Always has."

"Well, she doesn't scare me."

"You think I don't know that? You're a right pair, you two."

Barbara smiles and they both look away.

Junior paces back and forth on the sidewalk in front of them. The town police cruise by and he counts imaginary change and checks his imaginary watch. Denise turns her gaze back and gives Barbara the box she's been holding.

"Will you give this to her? Bill picked it out. It's to make up for her not being a bridesmaid. It's got lace and bows and ribbons and flowers, God knows what-all else. She won't be able to move. The crinoline is three feet wide."

"And I'm the one that will have to iron it."

"Tell her I'm sorry we didn't stay to say good-bye. I'd cry, that's all. It's these damn hormones."

"You want to let up on yourself."

Denise walks across the street to where Bill is waiting, gets in their car, gets out again. She walks over to Junior Maynes, jams a twenty in his hand, then gets back in the car. Bill drives up the dappled street, turns left at the lights and heads for the highway.


There is still some leftover birthday cake for Livy's after-school lunch. The new dress hangs on the pantry door so she can gloat over its yards of ruffle and lace as she eats. She peels off strips of icing, rolls them into candy balls, lines them up and eats them in order of size, smallest to largest.

When the cake is gone she carries the cookie jar over to the table. "I want to wear high heels like Denise. Great big ones."

"You'll break your neck."

"No I won't."

"You can't run in high heels and you like to run."

Livy thinks for a moment, squirrelling around in the jar for the cookie with the most chocolate chips. "Then I'll wear cowboy boots with big heels."

"Cowboys can't run."

"They can."

"No they can't. Their legs are bowed and they can't run a bit. That's why they ride horses." Barbara pours a glass of milk and sets it in front of Livy. "Ever think you might want to go live with Denise and Bill?"

Livy is astonished. "What for?"

"Well, so you'd have a mother *and* a father."

"No way! Jesus H. Christ!" Livy thumps her glass down, sloshing milk over her knuckles.

"Watch your mouth unless you want to talk through soapsuds." Barbara mops up the milk and wipes the bottom of the glass.

"You're not gonna make me live with them, are you?"

"Never. You're my girl. I was just curious."

Livy shoves her cheek against Barbara's hip, crunches her cookie hard and listens to the sound echo off Barbara's solid flesh. Suddenly she stops. "Wait! I forgot to show you!" She drags her knapsack up onto the table and pulls out a crumpled paper pinwheel. "It's for Bimbo. We have to stick it on his roof so the wind can blow it around."

"It'll get wet, Livy. It's going to rain any minute."

"But I want to. It's his birthday present."

"We'll make another one. We'll use this one for a pattern and we'll cut up your old raincoat."

They make four pinwheels of bright red plastic, attach them to barbecue skewers and, using fence staples and a hammer, mount one on each corner of the doghouse. The wind twirls them around. Bimbo barks.

"You're welcome, Bimbo," says Livy. "They're waterproof and everything."

"Let's get inside before this rain gets serious," says Barbara.

Livy hops up the steps backwards, then stops and throws herself on Barbara. She wraps her arms and legs around her aunt and hangs on.

"Take it easy," says Barbara.

The clouds split open and the rain begins to beat down, heavy drops that stamp the railing with big seals and soak the back of Barbara's green dress. Rain trickles down her bare arms and drips off her elbows as she carries Livy across the porch and into the house.

"You weigh a ton."

"Two tons," says Livy.

# Burning off the Heather

—◆—

"Did you call like I told you?"

"Mama says not to."

"Never mind what your mother says. You go on and call the fire department now. She's going to burn down the whole neighbourhood."

"I don't think so, Daddy. She's got the hose with her."

"That hose is less than a hundred feet long."

"She put another piece on it. It's plenty long." Sally patted him on the shoulder. "Don't worry."

"It's that damn Scottish blood of hers. First bit of warm weather and they go all queer in the head, want to burn the heather off the hills or something." Robert stuck his head out the back kitchen window and bellowed, "No heather out there, Meg! Damn crazy Scot!"

Meg, standing in the backyard in black rubber boots, Nicki's old ski jacket and a green and blue paisley head-scarf, waved a shushing hand at him and turned her back.

"Don't you be swearing at Mama. She's just tidying up the yard a little and burning the trash off the kitchen garden."

"That stuff's supposed to go on the compost pile to rot. I've shown her I don't know how many articles in the *Organic Gardening* magazine. It's her subscription, for Jesus' sake! I point them out to her, right there on the page, full-colour illustrations. Doesn't pay the slightest bit of attention. Pays for advice and then won't take it."

"She likes things to be tidy, that's all."

"No, she likes to set fires. Gets all dreamy and goosey staring at the flames. Watching them run away from her across the yard. Damn Scots blood."

"Call the fire department yourself, if you want. I'm going out to help her."

"Don't you get lippy. You've got that gene for burning up the countryside, too. I can see it in your eyes."

Sally grinned at her father, pulled a toque down over ruddy curls and slammed the door behind her. Robert watched the pair of them, setting little back fires, spraying lines of water to contain and direct the flames. The smoke billowed and swirled, puffing up in greenish grey balls whenever the fire reached a damp clump of weed stalks. The tree trunks at the edge of the back field shimmered through the lens of invisible rising heat. He pulled the rocking chair closer to the window so he could watch, took his coffee in one hand and sat down with the telephone perched on his knee. In case. He was supposed to be upstairs doing his taxes. Time was running out; it was almost the end of the month.

"How am I supposed to concentrate with a couple of pyromaniacs in the backyard?" he asked the cat. "Somebody's got to be responsible; somebody's got to keep an eye on those fools."

The cat blinked her amber eyes slowly and stared at him. Avoidance tactics, she seemed to say. Displacement activity. Anything to avoid those papers.

"Shut up," he said. "Smart-ass cat. I'd like to see you dial the fire department in an emergency."

She yawned, fanging her upper jaw at him.

Meg and Sally raked bits of straw the fire had skirted and threw them in the path of the meandering blaze. Behind it a fragile black mantilla of stems and leaves lay across the ground. Small breaths of wind crushed it to powder and puffed it up like tiny explosions.

"Daddy's having a fit. I think his nerves are gone."

"You'd think I set fire to the woods on a regular basis. It only happened once and we got it out before it went anywhere. That was twelve years ago, for pity's sake. A fluke wind. That man forgets nothing—if and when it suits him."

"So is he coming to the airport to see Nicki next week or what?"

"He hasn't decided."

"You mean you're still hoping he'll change his mind."

"Wait till you have kids. Just wait."

"You always say that. It's a hollow threat, Mama. If—and I mean if—I decide to have children, I certainly intend to do a better job than you and Daddy."

"You're not such a disaster, cookie. And neither is Nicki."

"That was a joke, Mama. Lighten up. Like your boots." Sally burst into giggles and directed the hose at Meg's smouldering heels.

At four-thirty Robert got up, opened a beer and began to cook supper: basmati rice and stir-fry. He diced and chopped, dropped heaping handfuls of onion, celery, mushrooms, carrot and broccoli into a sizzling cast-iron pot. Tossed in toasted almonds and slivers of marinated chicken. Turned everything down to low and called in his smoky womenfolk. They sat around the oval birch table, twined their feet around chair legs and ate like lumberjacks, charcoal smuts on their shirts and arms.

"Thank you, darling," said Meg. "This is delicious."

"Yeah, Daddy. Great meal." Sally wore a faint aroma of singed hair. A flip of the hose as she'd been chasing wayward flames had knocked her toque into the fire, and a stray spark had shortened one curl. Robert gazed at its frazzled end and was flooded with anxiety; he felt like a dry sponge thrown into a lake, abruptly saturated and sinking.

"Tomorrow we'll do the field east of the house," said Meg.

"And then? The whole eastern seaboard! Why stop there? Why not Central America? South America? Think Antarctica will burn?"

Sally was laughing at him. How could she be so beautiful? Why had he ever had children? He got up and scraped his plate into the compost bucket, then went outside. He stood on the porch watching, mistrusting the quiet, blackened field, then crossed the yard to his shed. He shifted a pile of rags, opened a tackle box and pulled out a package of cigarettes from the bottom drawer. Checked to make sure he'd hooked the door. Lit a cigarette. Smoked it slowly, deliberately. He was just lighting a second one when he heard Meg's quiet knock.

"Password," he said, shifting the cigarette behind his back and lifting up the hook.

"Sex, drugs, rock 'n' roll," she replied.

"Very funny." He opened the door and she slipped inside. He hooked it shut again. "Want a drag?"

"Oh, damn. Just one. Got any gum? Or breath mints?"

"All kinds."

Meg inhaled to her toes, grinned and flapped her arms. "Take it back or I'll smoke it all. Do you think she knows?"

"If she does she turns a blind and diplomatic eye. Pities her poor old weak-willed folks, hooked on a drug they just can't ever leave completely alone."

"If they were all like the first drag," mused Meg, "one shot and you're set. Doesn't this make you feel like you're twenty and smoking dope?"

"Makes me feel stupid."

They passed it back and forth until Meg said, "No, no more." She snuggled under his arm and ran her fingers under his shirt. "So let's talk about the other fire. And I don't mean me."

"What's to talk about?"

"Are you coming to the airport with us or not?"

Robert thought about lighting a third cigarette.

"Are you going to answer me or not?"

"You're a pushy woman. I don't want to go to the airport to

spend a half-hour with Nicki while she switches planes and flies off for the rest of her life. I want her to come home where she belongs."

"The rest of her life?"

"Well, who knows when she'll be back? And why is nineteen the legal age around here, anyway? What was wrong with twenty-one? Twenty-one was a perfectly reasonable number."

"You don't want to meet Louis."

"Why should I? Why the hell would I?"

Meg stepped back and stared directly into his eyes. He dropped the cigarette package and bent over to pick it up. Pulled out a third cigarette and struck three or four matches before he got it lit. "Must be wet or something," he said.

"My father," she said, "called Interpol about you."

"He what? When?"

"Mother woke up one night about a week after we flew to Amsterdam and found him on the phone, trying to convince some poor little receptionist on the other side of the Atlantic—God knows how he got the number—that their top agent should get off his butt and investigate you. He accused you of kidnapping a minor and hinted strongly that you might be an international drug dealer."

Robert's mouth opened and Meg lifted the cigarette from his lower lip. "Occasional cheating's one thing. Three in a row is over the line."

"But—your father likes me. We get along fine."

"Now. The summer you and I took off to bum around Europe he wanted you in a foreign jail with sewage running down the walls. Castrated with a rusty butter knife."

"But we were older than Nicki is. Maybe not that much older, OK, I give you that—but we'd known each other longer. And Meg, the world's a much more dangerous place these days."

"I try very hard not to think about that."

"That's a hell of an attitude—just don't think about it and everything will be fine?"

"It works as often as it doesn't. Which means I'm only scared out of my mind about half the time. What's the point in having children if you won't let them grow up? Do you want to lock her up in her room until she turns thirty?"

"That sounds good. All right, let's do that."

"Robert!"

"Don't lecture me, Meggie. I know all that crap. It's just, I'm not cut out to be a parent."

"Whoops! Too late."

"I can't handle the stress."

"It will be easier with Sally."

"No it won't. It'll be worse. To the power of ten."

"We've been telling the girls our travelling stories since they wore pyjamas with feet; just what did you expect was going to happen? You can't tell me you didn't see this coming."

"We didn't see a tenth of what was in front of us. Too busy drinking cheap wine and making love."

"Get with the tour, Robert. Nicki is twenty; she's going rambling for the summer with her boyfriend. They'll drink buckets of wine and make love until they can't walk. Five or six years from now it'll be Sally. No fire department in the world can put out that blaze for you."

"He really called Interpol?"

"Twice, actually."

"I'll be damned." Robert pulled her in close and rubbed his chin in her smoky hair—Sally's red with silver wings. "Does he still have the number, do you think? Oh, I'll go, I'll go to the damn airport. But I won't like it. And I won't like him."

"But you'll be civil."

"I won't spit on him." He found her mouth and opened it with his tongue. She was kissing him and smiling and snaking her hands under his belt.

There was a rattle and a bang as Sally kicked at the door from the outside.

"Childus interruptus," sighed Meg.

"We never learn," he agreed. He raised his voice: "Now what?"

"The fire's flared up," yelled Sally. "Quit necking or fighting or whatever and help me stomp it out."

Meg and Robert squeezed through the door frame together, legs tangled, trying to run.

"Didn't I tell you, you damn Scottish firebug!"

"Oh, hush up. And toss me a breath mint."

Crunching chlorophyll-laced candy, they arrived, breathless, to stomp and smother the teasing line of flames that was reaching for the woods. By the time they'd got the fire out, the sun was a primrose afterglow behind the trees. Sally trudged back and forth, scanning for stray wisps of smoke as Robert poured on the buckets of water Meg filled with the hose that didn't reach quite far enough.

"Those clouds are full of rain," Meg said. "It's going to pour any minute."

"Lucky for you, my dear."

"Planning, not luck. I did check the weather before lighting this thing. Give me credit for a little sense."

"Yeah, Daddy. Give the woman some credit here."

It was dark when they returned to the house. Meg and Sally went off together to clean up, sharing the bathroom: Meg, in the shower, quick and practical, oatmeal soap and pumice stone; Sally, sunk in a tub of scented mist, something with orange blossoms that crept down the hall and pricked his nose when Meg opened the door. Their voices murmured together, rose in laughter, fell back again. Robert, in his study, neatened piles of paper and rearranged them on his desk. He re-sharpened his pencils, to be ready for the morning. Wiped a little dust off the computer screen. He heard, with relief, the quiet steady drumming of rain soaking into the ground.

He knew that behind the cloud cover a full moon was rising, but not a glimmer of its light reached him. He cranked open the window and leaned his head and shoulders out, staring as hard as he could. The night was inky black. He wiped an arm over his face and head, smearing the rain, then shaded his eyes with his hand to keep the drops from blurring his vision. He couldn't see a thing.

When he was twenty-one the world, for a time, had split itself in two. There was Meg, things she touched, landscapes she moved through, music she liked, expressions she rolled on her tongue or knitted into her brow; there was other. Meg and not-Meg. Sounds so naive, he thought, too simple to be true, but it really was like that. Then the world had woven itself back together again in complicated and busy patterns. First Nicki. Then Little Sally Sunshine—now as tall as her mother and deeply offended if addressed by that old nickname. Work, friends, this awkward house they'd learned to love. The sheer drop of the back stairs had given Robert nightmares when the girls were small; he'd kept the doors at the top and bottom locked and nailed shut so they couldn't tumble down and break their necks. If you could see the years of comings and goings in this house, he thought, if they could be traced out and shown, like a time-lapse photograph of a Saturday night in downtown Toronto, they would fill the rooms and halls with a tapestried braid of such light and colour that you would be stuck like a moth, circling and threading through the bright woven strands, unable and unwilling to imagine any other existence.

The smell of wet ash pinched the scent of orange blossoms from his nostrils. The field would be a mess in the morning, wet and charred, stubbled and ugly. In a week's time the bright spring grass would burst through the scorched ground, elbowing and shoving its way to the light. It would be so very green, so brilliant, tender and alive. Everything would begin again.

# Looking for Whales

Edmonton airport, July '84.

We're packed into a huge rectangular lounge, plate glass facing the hot tarmac. Grey plastic seats are piled with sheepskin-lined denim jackets, bulky parcels, and equipment with collapsed legs. Everyone smokes; I roll Drum tobacco out of a can and light wooden matches with my thumbnail, pretentious ritual I've picked up working in theatre. Small children drum and kick at things; chocolate and Orange Crush make high-water marks on their faces. Behind us is a wide corridor that leads to a bar and bathrooms. A neon blue martini with a winking green olive hangs over the door to the bar. I'd like a beer but the place is full of men leaning into their drinks, looking bored and predatory. If I sit quietly with a draft and a book, someone will convince himself it is a pose meant to attract attention. Besides, I might miss the plane: it's three hours late and who knows when the announcement will come, and the flight and crew whisk away to Hay River, Norman Wells and Inuvik, leaving me behind fending off the suits. Eleven hours since I left Halifax and it will be nine more before I finally arrive, broad daylight at two in the morning, to look for breakfast in downtown Inuvik. And still I won't be where I'm going.

The next morning, or the one after, there is a ride in a Twin Otter to Tuktoyaktuk. Such noise, seats roped in place with dirty webbing. Tw'otter, the other passengers teach me to say. Below is a tapestry of blue lakes and green tundra.

My husband meets me at Tuk airport: a grey landing strip and a low, steel-roofed building. We ride, in the back of a truck, over to the harbour. The land is flat and completely treeless. The houses in the village are tumbled blocks, and in the distance, pingos swell modestly against the horizon.

Three of his friends from U of T, Professors Tom and Alvin and their assistant, a grad student called Lisa, come by with a bottle of Scotch to celebrate my arrival. We drink, squeezed into the galley, and when the Scotch is gone, Lisa makes coffee. She brings my husband a cup, milk-and-sugared to his taste, and says to me, "I don't know how you like yours."

"Black is fine," I say.

After a few days I fall into a rhythm. Sleep in a hammock in the hold of an old research vessel, mould and the ship's gentle knocking against the pier spiralling me down each night. Shop at the Hudson's Bay, cook meals for the crew. I am unofficial, doing an invented job, here only because I am convinced I cannot stand one more long summer alone. If I can't live without him for four months, how can he live without me? He has no answer so here I am, trying to be useful.

We have dinner occasionally at the Polar Shelf Base, a summer camp for scientists and their technicians. Bunk rooms, dining hall, mail drop, a kitchen where hair-netted women produce hearty meals. We sit at long tables with plastic tablecloths held down by enormous jars of ketchup, relish or jam. Sketches decorate the tablecloths: weather charts, the shape of a propeller, the molecular structure of #1 crude. Half the scientists won't sit with the other half. I laugh out loud and am shushed; it's a dog-eat-dog world in the land of grants, lab space and chopper time. Some have taken to hanging outside the pilots' bedroom, hoping to snag a barely awake flyer who might be coerced, coaxed or bribed into making just one more flight for one more sample. The pilots fly, fly, eat, sleep, fly. Other scientists fetch them coffee, offer to have their students do laundry for them.

Occasionally there are movies and we stay to watch. The windows must be completely covered to block out the sunlight. At least one reel will spill its film off in shiny black loops and must be patiently rewound. One evening the sun touches down for the first time. We stop the movie and rush outside to watch. The fireball sinks, pauses and flattens slightly on the tundra, then lifts free. Sunset/rise stretches halfway around the horizon. Crimson and fuchsia soar upwards. Nikons and Hasselblads point every which way; there is much fiddling with filters and wide-angle lenses. Gathering it all in on film so they can look at it later. I spin slowly from left to right, swing my head back, wishing desperately for a different kind of eye. A continuous screen, a 360-degree wrap. I want to see all the sky at once, take it whole and complete into myself. Instead I look through portholes that offer two overlapping strips of the world and it is not nearly enough.

On sunny afternoons I sit on the deck with clipboard and pen recording information for Lisa. Weight, length, sex. I mark numbers on small plastic bags and hand them to her. Into them she drops the earbones she has dug out of whitefish. Fish grow rings in their earbones, like trees. It's how you tell their age. Like trees. You have to kill them to find out how old they are. We trade a netful of earboneless fish for a haunch of caribou and I cut it into chunks small enough to fit into the boat-stove oven. We sometimes go visiting in the village; on the table: a roast of caribou, a pan of bannock, a bottle of hard liquor. Tea if you prefer. I develop a taste for caribou. I've never liked venison, rabbit, partridge. Too gamey, I say, too wild. Caribou is not like any of these. What is it like? Like caribou. I can't get enough of it.

Behind the Hudson's Bay aluminum cans roll back and forth, tinny in the wind. When the children come to visit we give them a drink each, then put the empties in the garbage. The garbage goes to the dump where the bags break or get torn open and the cans roll loose across the tundra. The children are merry and polite. They sit in a row on the stern and watch us work, occasionally breaking into giggles. We amuse and perplex them. Cutting up fish to dig out their earbones, then throwing the fish away. Lisa explains that the scientists want to know how many fish live in the harbour, how big they are, how old.

"Ask my grandfather," says Baby. "He knows."

The older siblings want to talk about cities. The girls grill me; they want to know what things cost. My jeans. My sweater. I tell them it's a cold and racist world down there and they smile and shake their heads; not for them it won't be.

Lisa's about my age, blond and energetic. She's on our boat often, working or visiting. The skipper and crew like her; they've been hanging around together since before I arrived. She doesn't seem to have a boyfriend; she flirts impartially with all the men. Sits on my husband's lap and pulls his hat down over his eyes. She's a good sport, my husband says, and she can hold her liquor. One day she flies to Herschel Island off the Yukon coast with one of her professors and wrangles a seat for me. People kindly take me places: survey trips by float plane up the coast and over to Banks Island, to Inuvik on the booze run, down the Mackenzie River by zodiac to check for stranded belugas. I climb aboard anything that moves. How can I turn any of this down? Each chance may be the only, the last.

At seven in the morning, Lisa, nine others and I climb into a twelve-seater helicopter. It's like a military bus with rotors. We sit in rows, wear headphones that don't begin to block out the noise. I'm deaf when we finally touch down. The plan is to pour oil onto the island and track it, to see what will happen if/when there is a large spill on the tundra. All around us are exquisite miniature flowers. "Arctic alpine," someone explains, taking samples and photographs. Nearby three others are emptying oil drums over the flowers in a large staked-out area.

I look for signs of the whaling station that was here in the late eighteen hundreds but there's nothing. The whalers didn't stay long. Too cold to overwinter, so they went back to killing from ships in the summertime. The only whale I've seen is a beluga washed up on the shore, flesh withered and foul on its bones. I pried a tooth loose with a long stick, then boiled it clean while the crew complained about the smell and the fact that I'd used the best saucepan. I cleaned the pan, pocketed the tooth.

It was such a small whale. Shot, died of its wounds, washed ashore to rot. Dead whales are a reproach—look at what we've done. There will be an accounting. I turn down the offer of whale meat one evening in the village. What's different? Other than that I've never heard a record of caribou singing?

By early September we are packed. Lisa and her professors have already gone, taking crates of samples and slides with them. Lisa was miserable, and cried when she said her good-byes. A blizzard rips across the water and we huddle around the stove in our parkas. The portholes are blind and frozen shut. The boat is hauled and we camp out at Polar Shelf until we can charter a flight out. The air is frigid as we drive to the harbour for the last time. The sun polishes everything; the Cessna floats on a silver mirror. When we're properly stowed and buckled the pilot jumps onto a pontoon and rocks the plane back and forth to break the surface tension so we can take off. We fan rooster tails across the water, lift free, and before I think to turn for a last look, we swing south and Tuk is lost in the distance. Long before we reach Inuvik the water will have healed. As if we'd never been.

Red Bay, Fall '84.

We move out of Halifax and rent an old boarding house down the coast. Once a place for travelling salesmen and plant workers from the abandoned whaling station up the road, it's been empty for a few years. It's too big, it's expensive to heat, but we fall in love with the view, and the location is right. We want to be out of the city; we've been talking for years about buying a place in the country, growing our own food, maybe having children. If we want, we can buy it.

"Let's spend a winter here first and see," he says. Maybe we can turn it into a bed and breakfast, and I can give up working in the costume department of the theatre with its crazy, unpredictable work schedule. We close off the upstairs wing with its corridor of bedrooms, numbers hand-lettered on the doors.

#4: the potato room.

We bring home potatoes after a weekend on P.E.I., the small mis-shapen ones the machines disdain. Bending over to gather them, I feel someone should be painting us, brushes recording my mud-stained jeans and the red paisley scarf tied around my head. It's an ancient scene: wheat, potatoes, rye, whatever falls to the ground and is left for those who come after. There should be a baby tied in a sling on my back. We fill the trunk of the car with far more potatoes than we can eat but we intend to plant some in the spring. Back at the boarding house, we spread them carefully on newspaper, each potato not touching its neighbour, in bedroom #4. In December it is so cold in the unheated upstairs wing that the starch in the potatoes turns to sugar. I have no idea such a thing can happen. They become inedible and I buy potatoes in the city. In January they will freeze solid; in the spring, thaw, turn black and rot. One Sunday in April I will carry boxes of them down the stairs and out to the compost pile. I will scrub the floor and leave the window open until the sweet-rot smell is gone.

#7: the dead room.

Wallpaper, faded blowsy roses, grey paint on the floorboards. Air will not circulate in this room. An overgrown apple tree fills the window with such a tangle of branches and suckers that the sun cannot creep in, even after the leaves have fallen. There is a smell, old earth and mouse droppings. I want nothing of mine in this room. I take the skeleton key and lock the door.

Every few evenings the postmistress calls to give me permission to come after hours for my mail. I seldom make it home from the city in time. "Your phone bill's here," she says, "and a new catalogue from Sears. There's a letter from your sister and a postcard from your aunt in Florida."

"She steams your mail open," says the guy at the garage.

"Do you think so?" I am horrified.

"You leave your mail there for days, 'course she does. What else has she got to do since they took out the party lines? We pick up our mail soon as the truck gets in from Halifax. Hell, my wife watches her sort it to see she don't squirrel some of it under the counter so's she can read it that night and make like it come in the next day."

Letters arrive. One, two, six, a dozen. By late fall they come three and four a week. I put them in a basket for my husband to open when he comes home, long white business envelopes with his name in bold loops and curves. He's working on an oil rig off the coast and is home one week in four. The basket sits on the living-room floor under a spider plant the cats have boxed into submission. He sets his coffee to cool, arranges his elbows to accommodate his newspaper. "Listen to this," he says, and I do, watering my plants, nodding and smiling as he comments. Later he reads one of the letters and pockets the rest.

"How is Lisa?" I ask. "Is she coming for a visit?"

"She's fine," he says. "No, she doesn't have any money."

December sleet drives past the windows; he can't get home and I have the flu. I sort the mail, throw a letter into the fire with the record club offers. When the next one arrives, I open the dead room and pitch it onto the floor. Lock the door. Hide the key. Winter drifts down around my head.

The living room:

big enough for a dance. Rows of windows on two sides. The moon reflects off the snow and fills the room with light. A grate from the furnace blows hot air. I shift from one bare foot to the other, brushing my wet hair into the flow as my nightgown billows.

The cats mill around the perimeter; they hate the feel of the metal grid on their paws. They stick their faces into the heat and complain. There is so much space here, I can spin like a top and bump into nothing. Run from one end of the house to the other and still miss a phone call.

"Let it ring a dozen times," I implore my friends. The cats run with me, eager to help or trip me. Which? Are they trying to sabotage the remnants of my social life? Keep me out in the country to open tins and doors for them?

#1: the MBR.

I decorate the room above the kitchen: wallpaper with blue cornflowers, eyelet curtains, a quilt of yellow and blue squares. I drink wine in bed as I read far too late into the night. Poetry, whatever is to be found on the shelves of the city library and the Book Room. Whales. The Big Book of. Humpback, fin, minke, right, blue, bowhead, sei—I memorize their names. When he comes home the bed is warmer and there is less room. When he leaves, empty hangers chime in the closet.

In the dead room, the pile is growing. The rustle of mice in the walls is the rustle of shifting, restless mail. The cats and I are on alert, ears pricked up so that our eyebrows always feel tight. One afternoon I slip into the dead room to poke and tap at the walls. The baseboards have pulled away just enough so that the letters will slide down behind them. I file the letters all around the room and when I have finished the room looks perfectly empty.

#6: the singing room.

Early in the fall, before the great potato freeze, I collect potatoes for a scallop; when I break into song, the room answers. Small potato eyes look up in astonishment. I test each room by singing scales. Sandwiched between the front and the dead room, #6 surrounds each note with silver. You would never guess its magic. Greyish yellow walls, crazed varnish, warped floorboards. The single window frames the cliff, picked out in seagulls and frilled with fast-moving clouds. I sing "Richland Woman Blues" and "Love Has No Pride," "Guilty" and "Love Me Like a Man." When winter bites down hard I wear hats and sweaters, close my eyes and sing until I shake with the cold and have to quit. Songs of love and betrayal, then the lover. Did one lead to the other, I wonder. Did I sing for so long and so passionately that there was no hope of escape? A student at Dalhousie, the stage manager's nephew, met at an opening-night party. I go to his apartment after work to eat takeout, share cigarettes and wine, make love until midnight. He never wakes when I get up, sprawls in the blue flannelette sheets his mother bought for him when he left home. He is long bones, tangled copper hair, dark Jesus eyes and a compelling sexual energy. I kiss his neck and cover him before I leave. Drive home in a stew of self-pity because it is not my husband who flashes with desire when I smile over my shoulder at him.

On a shelf in the costume department of the theatre is an old bundle of whalebone. We are building corsets for an Edwardian play, moulding the women into the shape of pouter pigeons with unbleached cotton and lengths of plastic-coated steel.

"Why don't we use this?" I finger the brownish strips, microplankton filters of a long-dead whale. Thom takes a piece and bends it; it snaps and splinters.

"Too old and dry." He holds up the jagged edges. "Imagine this cutting through fabric and skin. It was much better to work with; steel doesn't move or shape like whalebone. But you can't get it anymore."

We work late for a week to be ready for the first dress rehearsal and my student comes by to pick me up after the library closes. One night after everyone has gone, he laces me into a corset and we play a merry game of "Young Fergus from the village makes a delivery to the manor and comes upon the Mistress alone in her petticoats and corset and they are swept awae bye the force of theyre passione." Halfway through the game we have to stop and unlace the corset.

"How did people have sex in these things?" I ask the next day. "How could they breathe?"

"Didn't," says Thom. "Madame retired first; her maid unlaced her and dressed her in a loose robe. It takes at least half an hour for the pressure marks to fade from your skin. Not very attractive."

"But in the movies they're always rolling in the hay in their corsets."

"Movies!" sniffs Thom, threading a steel bone into its tight casing.

A surprising number of the actresses love their corsets. I can't lace them tight enough to suit. Their waists get squashed in and their breasts get shoved and mounded up under their chins. Veritable peaches. Melons, even. They pirouette before the mirrors, come-hither their reflections. I begin to suspect I am not the only one who has played "The Mistress and Young Fergus."

In the spring, I break with my student and leave my husband. I spend the last weekend at the house alone, dividing my time between packing and walking the cliffs. I wander as far as the old factory where a broken wharf of splintered creosote timbers sticks up in the tidewash. Under mounds grown over with turf and bramble are earth-stained bones: vertebrae as large as my pelvis, as small as my fist. Ribs that would have arched over my head. Spring-melt has uncovered a few of these bones and I dig out a small vertebra to pack away with my beluga tooth. No whales are to be seen.